DEAD MAN'S HAND

Johnny looked down at his cards and knew he had a winning hand. He looked across the table at the drummer from Omaha.

"Raise you ten," he said, tossing a gold eagle in the pot.

"All right," the drummer said, his moustache twitching. "I'll see your ten and raise you, uh, five."

This was going to be easy. Johnny glanced at the faces of the other players.

But they weren't looking at him; they were looking behind him. Johnny started to turn to see what they were looking at. A man's voice, cold, deadly, came from behind.

"Sit right still, mister gamblin' man."

Johnny felt the bore of a gun touch his back, right between the shoulder blades. His spine turned to ice. His voice wavered. "What . . . what is this, a robbery?"

"No, mister gamblin' man. It's a hangin'. You spoiled our party last night, and now we're gonna hang you."

DOYLE TRENT
GAMBLER'S GUNS

ZEBRA BOOKS
KENSINGTON PUBLISHING CORP.

ZEBRA BOOKS

are published by

Kensington Publishing Corp.
475 Park Avenue South
New York, NY 10016

First Printing: March, 1993

Printed in the United States of America

Chapter One

It was the ratcheting sound of a gun being cocked that froze the kid in his tracks. His spine suddenly went cold and stiff. The hair on the back of his neck turned to frost. The hunger that had been gnawing at his insides was forgotten. He was afraid to move, afraid to breathe.

The smell of smoke and cooking meat had brought him here to the edge of the woods. He was risking his life coming here. There were men who wanted to kill him. There were marauding Indians who hated white eyes. Slowly, holding his breath, he started to turn.

"Stand right still, mister." The voice was harsh, threatening. It was the voice of a white man. That was something of a relief. But it could belong to one of the Nash boys.

With fear making his heart pound, he said, "I ain't got no gun. I didn't mean no harm."

"Turn around, and keep your hands in sight.

Make a sudden move and this cannon will blow a hole in you."

The man with the gun was plump, with a round face and a trimmed gray beard. He was no one the youngster had ever seen before. But the face wasn't friendly, and the hogleg pistol in his hand was ugly and menacing. "What are you doing here? Who are you?"

Still fearful, he answered, "I—I'm just followin' the river, hopin' to find a road."

"You alone?"

"Yessir."

"Why are you afoot?"

"I ain't got no horse. I started out walkin' and got lost when it rained and I couldn't see the sun or the mountains."

"Where'd you come from?"

"Rollinsville."

"The law after you?"

"I ain't done nothin' wrong."

The plump man looked him over in the fading light of dusk. What he saw was a tall, skinny youth with sun-bleached hair showing under a shapeless black hat, a kid in ragged overalls and worn brogan shoes. "All right. Go that way." He pointed into the dense woods that grew along the South Platte River, a mixture of cottonwoods, locust, maple, and willow brush. He yelled, "It's all right, Jake. Just a lost kid."

The kid had to part the brush and tree limbs with both hands to make his way to a half-acre clearing on the bank of the river. There he saw the campfire and the frying meat that had drawn him here. He also saw another man, a man as tall as he was and not much heavier. The man had a rifle in his hands, a breech loader. Two bay horses hopped awkwardly with hobbled forefeet as they grazed on tall wheat grass.

"He's alone and he doesn't appear to be armed," the plump man said.

"Who is he, and whar'd he come from?"

"Says he's from Rollinsville. I've heard of it. It's a two-bit farmer town over east."

"What's he doin' here?"

"Says he's trying to find the road. Says he got lost."

Scowling, the tall one looked him over, asked, "What's your name, kid?"

"John Vorhes."

"How old're you?"

"Seventeen, sir."

"You're runnin' from somebody, ain't you?"

John Vorhes couldn't think of a quick lie, so he told the truth. "I hit a man and ran."

"Who'd you hit?"

"Mr. Nash. I been workin' for him and his sons."

"What kind of work?"

"We was brandin' cattle."

"What'd you hit 'im with?"

"Just my fist. I only hit 'im once."

"Just your fist, huh? Is that the truth?"

"Yessir." It was the truth.

The tall man leaned his rifle against a tree and squatted in front of the fire. He used a long-bladed skinning knife to turn over some meat sizzling in an iron skillet. The kid's knees went weak at the sight and smell of the frying meat. Looking from under a flat-brim black hat, the tall one said, "How long since you et?"

"Three days, sir."

"Set. We'll eat."

The plump man let the hammer down on his big pistol and jabbed it into a worn leather holster strapped waist-high on his right side. He dropped to the ground near the fire and sat cross-legged. "Old Jake shot an antelope this morning. We've got plenty of meat. Pull up a stump and sit."

Sitting cross-legged too, John Vorhes couldn't take his eyes off the frying pan. Jake turned a thin steak over again, then held it out to him on the end of the knife. "It's hot. I cut it off the shoulder. That's the best part. Blow on it." The kid had to toss the meat back and forth from one hand to the other until it cooled enough that he could take a bite. It was burned on the outside, but pink in the middle. Chewing rapidly, swallowing, he ate.

"If you haven't eaten in three days, your stomach won't handle too much too fast," the plump one said. "Better chew it thoroughly."

With a grin, the kid took another bite, half-tearing the meat apart with his teeth. Jake stood, went to a skinned and gutted antelope carcass hanging from a cottonwood limb, and sliced off another steak. The plump one stood, too, broke some dead branches off a willow tree, and added them to the fire.

"We're taking a gamble, making ourselves so visible," he said. "The Army hasn't run off all the Cheyenne and Kiowa yet."

"We gotta have a fire," Jake allowed. "We can't chaw raw meat."

John Vorhes was too busy eating to worry about Indians. He finished that steak and eyed the other two in the frying pan. Jake reached into a small cotton bag behind him, then threw a pinch of salt over the meat. "Only Injuns can eat without salt."

8

Now that he was no longer starving, the kid took notice of the two men and their camp. The plump one wore brown cotton pants held up with leather suspenders. He had jackboots on his feet and a dirty gray hat on his head. When he pushed the hat back, a sheaf of gray hair fell across his forehead. Pale blue eyes were set far apart in the round face. The face was pink, and didn't appear to be as well worn as the faces of most men his age. Jake was the opposite—tall, dark with a wrinkled rawhide face, and a brooding look about him.

Their camp was simple, two blanket rolls, two pairs of saddlebags, two saddles and bridles, two thick saddle blankets.

They ate steaks and slices of stale bread, then stomped out the fire. Without it, it was dark. A small light flared for a second as Jake set fire to a hand-rolled cigarette. "Smoke, kid?"

"Nossir. Thanks just the same."

"Neither does Bert. He don't smoke, chew, drink likker, or nothin'. He's edicated."

The kid said nothing to that. All Bert said was, "I've got two blankets. You can borrow one."

Jake stood. "I'm gonna look at the hosses. Be right back."

With a wool blanket wrapped around him, the kid slept better than he had in the past three nights. He felt safe in the dark, with two well-armed men on each side of him.

Safe until daylight, anyhow.

Breakfast was the same as supper the night before. But it was filling, and John Vorhes felt strong enough to travel on. "How far is it to the road that goes to Cheyenne," he asked.

9

"Only a few miles," Bert answered. "Do you know someone in Cheyenne?"

"My sister lives there. She married a feller in Rollinsville and they moved to Cheyenne."

"Oh. Well, you can catch a ride on a freight wagon sooner or later. I take it you don't have the price of a stage ticket."

"Nossir. I ain't got nothin'."

"Well, we'll fry you a couple more steaks that you can carry in your pocket and eat cold. You won't starve."

"Nossir. My poppa useta say a man could go a long time without eatin' if he had water, and that river water ain't too bad."

"Where's your poppa?"

"He's dead."

"Oh." The two men saddled their horses, rolled up their blankets, and packed their saddlebags. The kid said, "I sure do thank you. I would've starved if you hadn't've gave me some grub."

Mounted, Bert said, "You'll be all right now, kid. It's only a few miles to the road, and there's plenty of traffic. Folks are leaving Denver and heading for Cheyenne by the hundreds."

"In a few years," Jake said, "they can travel on the railroad—them that can pay."

He watched them ride away, going west, and he started walking, also going west. He followed the South Platte, staying close to the jungle of trees and brush that lined the river. While he walked, he repeatedly looked behind him, looked all around. The Nash gang would be on horseback, easy to see. He'd hidden from them along the river before. If necessary, he could hide in the brush again . . . he hoped.

The country was mostly flat, with a few long, low hills. The only trees grew along the creeks and in the low spots where water gathered in the wet seasons. The Nashes would ride many miles, checking every clump of trees and brush. Away over west, the Rocky Mountains drew a jagged, hazy, purple line across the horizon. Walking down here on the prairie, on the blue grama and buffalo grass, was easy.

John Vorhes tried to whistle a tune as he walked. He'd kept out of sight of the Nashes for three days and four nights now. And he hadn't seen any Indians. In a couple of days, if nothing happened, he'd be in Cheyenne. He'd find Suzanne, and they'd be happy to see each other. He'd borrow some money from her and her husband and get far away. Somewhere he'd get a job and then he could repay them.

It was mid-morning when he saw the road. There was no traffic in sight, but he believed someone would come along in a wagon, going north, and he could get a ride. He'd stay close to the river until he heard a wagon coming. But instead of hearing a wagon, he heard his name called: "Hey, kid. John . . . Johnny."

It was Bert and Jake, sitting their horses back in the trees next to the river. "Com'ere, will you?" He turned his steps in their direction.

"Need you to do somethin' for us, kid. Not much, just hang onto these ponies for a little while. Stay out of sight of the road."

"How come?"

The plump Bert answered, "It's better to have someone hold the horses than to tie them up. Tied horses sometimes get excited and break loose."

"Where're you goin'?"

"Don't ask no more questions. Will you do it?"

"Sure."

The two men handed him their reins, then started taking off their clothes. John Vorhes watched them, puzzled. He wanted to ask why they were doing that, but kept his mouth shut when Bert said, "Don't ask."

Stripped to their long underwear, they took off their hats and put on ragged bill caps with earflaps, the kind some men wore in the winter. They wrapped bandanas loosely around their throats. "Stay here, kid," the tall Jake said. "No matter what happens, stay right here, out of sight."

They walked away carrying only their guns. Suddenly, when they were near the road, they ducked back into the trees and brush. The kid was so curious he almost couldn't stand it, but he did as he was told and stayed out of sight. He heard horses coming from the south, several horses, traveling at a trot. He heard their hoofbeats, heard trace chains rattle, heard a wagon creak.

Heard a gunshot.

Men were yelling. Another shot. More yelling. Quiet for a long moment. Then the horses and coach were going away at a gallop.

Footsteps. Running. Bert and Jake came crashing into the brush, carrying a heavy canvas bag. Moving fast, they put on their clothes, threw away the caps, and put on their hats. Bert reached into the bag and took out a gold coin and handed it to the kid.

"Here, Johnny. It's ten dollars. Take it, and don't say anything about us. You didn't see us or ever hear of us."

"Yeah, kid," Jake said. "We done you a favor,

and now you owe us one. You didn't see nothin' or hear nothin'."

"Y-yessir," the kid said. He watched them mount and ride away at a lope, going southeast. It was easy to figure out what had happened.

They'd just robbed the stage.

Chapter Two

Johnny Vorhes rolled out of bed and pulled on his polished calfskin boots. Daylight was showing in the second-floor window of his hotel room. He went to the window, raised the shade halfway, and looked down on a dusty street of Cheyenne in the new Territory of Wyoming. An early-morning sun was casting long shadows on the street. Wagon after wagon went past, carrying lumber, rolls of tarpaper and kegs of nails. The city was growing at the rate of over a thousand people per month. Houses were going up everywhere. Over east, a steam whistle summoned railroad builders to the work train. The Denver Pacific was building south at a rapid rate.

Cheyenne was a good town for a gambling man.

Behind him, the young woman known as Frankie mumbled something in her sleep, turned over on her side, and resumed snoring lightly. Suddenly her blue eyes opened. "You're up already?"

"It's a longtime habit," Johnny said. He sat on

the edge of the bed and shoved his booted feet into the legs of good wool pants. Standing, he tucked the tail of his white pleated shirt into the pants. "Sometimes I wish I could break that habit."

"We didn't go to bed until . . . what was it, three o'clock? My last performance was at ten, and your card game didn't break up until after one."

"Yeah, and I know those gents are gonna be there again tonight, just itching to win their money back. I wish I could sleep later. I could use more sleep."

He washed his face out of a china basin and combed thick, dark brown hair. Looking at himself in a wood-framed mirror, he grimaced and wished he hadn't broken that tooth when he was a kid. The chipped tooth, right in front, detracted from what would have been a handsome smile. Detracted from it, but didn't ruin it.

He'd filled out in the past three years. No longer was he the skinny, gangly kid in ragged clothes with bleached hair and a sun-peeled nose. But he could still be recognized. Maybe not at first glance, but anyone who had known him three years ago and who took a good look now would recognize him.

"Well, don't expect me to get up so early. I've got two performances tonight."

Forcing a grin, Johnny said, "I thought you were raised on a farm in Iowa. Farm girls get up early."

"Not this one. Not no more." Frankie rolled onto her stomach, turned her face to the wall, and let one bare arm dangle over the side of the bed. It was a shapely arm. She was a shapely young woman. Short blond hair, bright blue eyes. A little hard, a little tough, but pure female.

"I'll eat breakfast and go over to the barbershop for a shave," Johnny said, putting on his homburg. "See you later."

15

No more eating at the Ford restaurant, where working men lined up at a long counter like hogs at a trough. Instead, Johnny Vorhes seated himself at a table at Reuben's Fine Foods, ordered coffee, eggs, and hotcakes, and unfolded the latest issue of the *Rocky Mountain Star*. Another shooting, a headline said. Police Chief Tobias Wimmer wanted the municipal council to pass an ordinance outlawing guns in the city. Johnny snorted. They could pass all the laws they wanted to, but there'd still be shootings, stabbings, and clubbings. Cheyenne didn't get the nickname "Hell on Wheels" for nothing.

He read every headline hopefully, and was disappointed for the hundredth time. No story about the Nash brothers being shot or hung or sent to prison. No news was bad news.

His meal finished, he was on his second cup of coffee when Bertram Goodfellow came in and dropped his plump body into a chair across the table. Bertram hadn't aged at all. His round face still had few wrinkles, and his gray beard was always neatly trimmed. Only now he dressed like a millionaire. He had to. As owner of Goodfellow's Fine Clothing for Ladies and Gentlemen, he had to advertise his own products.

"Saw Jake last night," he said, matter-of-factly.

Putting his coffee cup down, Johnny asked, "How is Jake these days?"

"He's broke and looking for action. I gave him a few dollars, but he's looking." Bertram glanced around to make sure no one could overhear him, and added, "He's got an idea. He's going to do some more checking, and if it's as good as he thinks it is, he'll need us."

"Things are changing, Bert. That vigilance committee is hanging folks."

"I know it. We can't take reckless chances like we used to."

"Did Jake say what he's got in mind?"

"Wouldn't say yet. Said he's going to do some riding and checking."

"I hope he's not too desperate."

"I warned him that you and I don't intend to get caught." Bertram ordered breakfast from a waitress who wore a long white apron tied with a big bow at the back. When she left, he said, "Hear you're taking up with that actress, the blond one named Frankie."

"Yeah. She likes to sleep late."

"You have to be careful what you say to her. Don't talk in your sleep."

Johnny Vorhes only grinned.

After he left the barbershop, smelling of lilac water, he strolled down the plank walk and enjoyed the midsummer air. From a few tents pitched ahead of the coming railroad, Cheyenne had grown to a city with everything. There were stores ranging from gunshops to haberdasheries. There were three variety theatres, including the Soiled Dove, where Frankie performed with a troupe from St. Louis. There were two banks, two newspapers, a post office, a telegraph office, restaurants, hotels, and at least a half-dozen saloons.

Most of the railroad builders went on west with the Union Pacific, but some stayed and were now working on the southbound Denver Pacific. There were soldiers from Fort Russell and Camp Carlin mixing on the sidewalks with well-dressed businessmen and denim-clad working men. A few cowboys had been seen in the saloons, now that Texas cattlemen had discovered the good grazing lands of Wyoming Territory.

And there were professional gamblers, like Johnny Vorhes.

He walked past the Red Ox, where a bartender had once started to chase him out, then allowed him to make a sandwich from the free lunch counter. Music from a big barrel organ reached the sidewalk, but was drowned out by the creaking freight wagons and the hammering from a blacksmith shop. He walked past the Dodge House, where he'd spent his first few nights, sharing beds with strangers in a room that held about thirty beds. He remembered waking up with a start, scared, every time someone entered the room.

He remembered the towels and combs used by everyone, and how he'd pulled the towel around on its roller, looking for a clean spot.

And the bearded gent who'd got out of bed in his long underwear, pulled the one blanket down, and yelled, "Gawdam, thar's livestock in this gawdam bed."

"Ain't neither," the proprietor had yelled back, "unless you brung 'em."

Johnny walked on. Life had been good lately. His only disappointment was that he hadn't found Suzanne. He'd tried. He'd asked the police chief to help, but was roughly dismissed. He'd even knocked on doors, asking. No one had heard of an Alan Mitchell or a Mrs. Alan Mitchell. He'd traveled by stage to Denver and spent four days asking there. He had to find her. She knew about Poppa's death, but she didn't know that Momma had died later. It was the hope of eventually finding his sister that kept him here. Were it not for her, he'd be far away, clear out of the Nash bunch's territory. Suzanne was the only family he had left. They'd been very close as kids. She'd do anything for him. And he'd do anything, risk anything, to find her.

And at the same time, he had to keep watching—warily watching.

They wouldn't give up. They were duty-bound to kill him. He'd killed one of them.

With nothing else to do, he went back to his room at the Cheyenne Arms. Frankie was still in bed, but she woke up when he entered. He envied her ability to sleep late.

"Umph," Frankie said.

Johnny sat on the side of the bed and pulled off his boots. He lay on his back and closed his eyes, trying to sleep. A poker player had to be able to play all night and stay wide awake. A man who got drowsy soon found himself broke. Frankie said, "Say Johnny, will you do me a favor?"

"Umph."

"Will you take my bladder to the water closet and drain it for me?"

"Umph."

"Well, then I guess I'll have to do it myself." Frankie crawled out on the opposite side, wearing her long, silky nightgown with thin straps holding the top over her breasts. Johnny's eyes came open to watch her breasts jiggle as she moved about.

"Say, maybe we could . . ."

"Forget it. Now that I'm up I'm gonna stay up."

"Maybe I could sleep some afterward."

"Huh-uh. That water closet is calling." She slipped her arms into a long wool robe, belted it, ran her fingers through her short blond hair. She opened the door a crack, peered into the hall, then slipped out.

Johnny grinned. Every man in town would pay

plenty to see Frankie the way he'd seen her. All they could do was try to imagine how she looked with nothing—absolutely nothing—on. Every night they packed the Soiled Dove to see her and her troupe. The St. Louis Art Players, they called themselves. They sang and danced, and comedians with false noses and baggy pants told jokes. The crowd whistled and yelled when the girls did the French Can-Can.

But what brought the house down was Frankie's act. In a comedy skit, a buffoon "accidentally" grabbed the back of her dress and pulled it off. She was left standing there on the stage in her skintight knee-length drawers, and so little covering her breasts that all but the nipples showed. She had practiced looking shocked and embarrassed until she had it perfected. And when she scurried around the stage, frantically looking for something to put on, a hush came over the crowd. Men stared, open-mouthed—until she pranced off the stage. Then they howled, whistled, clapped their hands, and stamped their feet.

A Union Pacific magnate had offered her fifty dollars to go to bed with him. When she refused, he offered her a hundred dollars. When she refused that, he proposed marriage and promised to build her the biggest and finest house in town.

She chose the quiet, moody Johnny Vorhes instead, and he'd offered her nothing.

Lying on his back, hands under his head, he grinned at the ceiling. Yeah, life had been good. He had everything. And he was only twenty.

But . . . there was that constant nagging ache at the back of his mind. It could all end suddenly. When he thought about it, he knew it would end.

He tried not to think about it.

Frankie came back and said she was going to her own room down the hall, and she would have breakfast alone or with members of her troupe. "We can't keep it a secret that we're sleeping together," she said, "but there's no use flaunting it."

He agreed, and turned over on his side and tried to sleep. He couldn't. Finally he got up, pulled on his boots, combed his hair, put on his hat, and went down on the street. One of the first men he saw was Jason Bowers.

"I'll see you in the Silver Bell tonight," the fat, well dressed Bowers said.

"Sure."

The fat man's voice was threatening. "You better be there, and you better bring all the money you took from us last night. And then some. I'll bring the cards. Tonight I'm gonna clean you out and run you outa town."

Chapter Three

Jason Bowers owned the slaughterhouse and the butcher shop, and he made more money than he knew what to do with. When he first went into business in Cheyenne, while the railroad was stalled for the winter at Hillsdale, he sold T-bone steaks for 12½ cents a pound. Wild meat went for 10 cents a pound, and half an antelope cost only $1.50. Then the railroad got to Cheyenne, bringing hordes of people with it. Jason Bowers doubled his prices and got rich.

He was married to a woman who was as fat as he was, but he didn't spend much time at home. He liked to play cards, so he was in the Silver Bell Gaming Parlour every night. Trouble was, he hated to lose. Everyone knew he carried a nickel-plated, double-action revolver in a shoulder holster under his coat, and no one doubted he'd use it if he thought he was being cheated.

Johnny Vorhes didn't doubt it. Just the same, he was now looking level-eyed across the round table at Bowers. He said, "Mr. Bowers, anybody that can't stand to lose oughtn't to play cards."

Bowers' eyes were mere slits as he watched the kid rake in the pot. He repeated, "I said, gimme them goddam cards."

The Silver Bell was the fanciest gaming house in town, with glass chandeliers hanging from the ceiling, red velvet covering on the walls, a polished mahogany bar, sawdust on the floor, and gaming tables of all kinds, including a faro table and a roulette wheel. An iron railroad bell, painted silver, hung at the far end of the room. The proprietor had taken the clapper out. Too many men had rung the bell just to make a noise.

Johnny shoved his cards across a felt-lined table occupied by five men. The fat man picked them up one at a time and studied them carefully. He said, "Turn your left hand over. Turn it over, goddam it." Johnny turned his hands over, palms up. They were empty. He didn't even wear a ring. Glancing at the other three men at the table, Bowers growled, "Roll up your sleeves."

"I don't like what you're trying to accuse me of, Mr. Bowers, but just to save trouble, all right." Johnny unbuttoned the cuffs of his white pleated shirt and pulled up the sleeves. He couldn't keep the agitation out of his voice when he said, "Satisfied? Or do you wanta look under the table?"

"Yes, by God, I'll do that, too."

"Maybe we oughta quit now. I don't think I want to play with you anymore, Mr. Bowers."

The businessman growled, "No, by God, you ain't quittin'. You ain't quittin' till I say you can." He shoved back his chair, stood, and came over to Johnny's side of the table. "Git outa the way. Let's just have a look."

Johnny knew what he was looking for—a bug, a simple length of watchspring fastened to the underside of the table with a tack. A player could hold his cards on end in front of him to hide his movements and slip an ace or a king between the spring and the underside of the table. Sooner or later the card would be what he needed to fill a straight or an ace-high full house. Bowers found no bug.

While he was looking under the table, Johnny patted his stomach, reassuring himself that the little two-shot .41 was there in a specially made holster, out of sight behind the waistband of his wool pants. "Well?" he demanded when the fat man straightened up.

"Just deal the goddam cards." Bowers sat again, and Johnny gathered the cards and started to shuffle. "Wait a minute. Wait just a goddam minute." Bowers pulled a deck of Broadway playing cards out of his coat pocket. "Use these."

Looking at the other men, Johnny asked, "Any objections?" There were none. Johnny spread the cards across the table, removed the jokers, counted the face cards, then gathered them and shuffled with practiced fingers. "Five-card draw," he said. He dealt each man five cards, then studied their faces as they picked up their hands. No one changed expressions. Sam Knolls, owner of a freight line, swallowed, but Johnny figured that didn't mean anything. Bets were tossed into the center of the table. "Cards, gentlemen?"

A cowboy from Texas who wore spurs on his boots and spoke with a slow drawl sat on Johnny's left. He threw down two cards. Johnny dealt him two. Sam stayed pat, meaning he either had a full house or better or he wanted everyone to think he did. The next man threw down three cards. He had two of a kind and hoped to draw a third or at least two pair. Bowers threw down two cards. He had three of a kind and was hoping for a full house. Only then did Johnny look at his cards. He had the king of spades and absolutely nothing else to build on. He dealt himself four cards. "Bets?" More money, both greenbacks and coins, were tossed onto the table.

"Raise you fifty," Bowers growled, carefully placing five gold eagles on the table and looking at the faces around him. Johnny had the odds memorized. The chances of Bowers improving his hand by drawing two cards were one in nine. The cowboy turned his cards face down. "Too rich for my blood." Sam called. He hoped Bowers was bluffing. The fact that he didn't raise was a pretty good indication that he wasn't sure of himself. The third man turned his cards down. "Whatever you got it beats what I got," he grumbled. Johnny looked at his cards. Two kings, two nines, and a deuce. It wouldn't beat Bowers' three of a kind. But the fat man liked to bluff, too. Johnny put four double eagles on the table. "Raise you thirty."

He knew from the look on the fat man's face that he'd outbluffed him. The only one he had to worry about now was Sam. "Whatta you say, Sam'l?"

Sam studied his cards, the pile of money in the center of the table, the money in front of him. And Johnny knew he'd won the pot with a little old two pairs. "Mr. Bowers?"

"Goddam it." Bowers threw down his hand. "You

knew what I had. You knew it all along." Sam turned his cards face down. "My hand ain't that good."

"Well," Bowers growled, "we by God paid to see what you got. Turn 'em over."

Johnny put his cards down face up, and reached for the pot. Bowers exploded.

"No, by God, you don't. Nobody wins a pot with two sorry little pairs unless he's cheatin'." He hooked his thumbs inside the armholes in his brocaded vest. His right hand was close to the butt of the nickel-plated revolver.

Anger that had been building in Johnny was close to boiling now. He had a powerful urge to jump up and smash that fat, hateful, insulting face. But he forced himself to calm down. As Bertram Goodfellow had often said, the man who keeps his wits about him wins. The wild, crazy ones lose.

"Listen, Mr. Bowers, you know poker is more than luck. It's a game of bluff. I outbluffed you. That's all there is to it."

"No, by God, there's more to it than that. I don't know how you done it, but you knew what I had in my hand. You're a pipsqueak, smartass dandy kid that never done an honest day's work in your life, and you ain't cheatin' me."

That did it. Johnny hissed between tight lips, "I did more honest labor by the time I was seventeen than you ever did in your whole goddam life, and I never cheated anybody. You're nothing but a bigmouth pile of shit."

Guns boomed.

Bowers was the first to fire. His right hand moved surprisingly fast, and he had the nickel-plated revolver out of its holster and pointed at Johnny's middle before Johnny could jump up. A metallic center-fire cartridge exploded just as Johnny threw himself to one side. The lead slug slammed into the wall at Johnny's back.

The fat man was crazy with anger. He half-stood, yanked the trigger again, missed again. Johnny's right hand darted inside the waistband of his pants.

It was a fast draw he'd practiced many times. The first part of his hand to touch the gun was his thumb on the hammer. In one fast, smooth motion he had his hand around the butt, a finger on the trigger, the hammer back, and the gun leveled at the man in front of him. The short-barreled .41 boomed once.

Gunfire was ringing in everyone's ears as the fat businessman sat down suddenly. His eyes went wide with shock and surprise. A red spot appeared on the left side of his chest. No one else moved as he dropped his pistol, slowly tipped sideways, and fell onto the floor.

It was quiet in the Silver Bell Gaming Parlour. For a long moment, everyone was frozen in place. Then Johnny Vorhes let the hammer down on the two-shot pistol and put it back inside his waistband. He reached for the money in the center of the table, but stiffened when he felt the bore of a gun pressed into the back of his neck.

"Leave it," a hard voice said. "Get your hands up."

Without looking back, Johnny raised his hands. "Step away from the table," the voice commanded. Johnny stepped back, turned. He found himself looking into the squinty eyes of Police Chief Tobias Wimmer. The lawman wore no uniform, but he had a small silver shield pinned to his vest, and he had a big six-shooter in his right hand.

"Did you see what happened?" Johnny asked.

"I saw you shoot that man, that Mr. Bowers. We don't take kindly to cardsharps and gunslingers. Keep your hands up now and don't move a muscle."

"I had to shoot him or get shot. There are all kinds of witnesses."

"Just the same, you're goin' to the hoosegow." The lawman found the .41, pocketed it. "Evidence. So's this." With his left hand he grabbed money from the table and stuffed it in his pockets. Soon he had his pockets full with all the money from the table. The Texas cowboy protested, "Say, that's my stake!" Growling, the policeman said, "Shut up, or I'll arrest you, too, for bein' an accessory or so-methin'. This is evidence."

"But . . ."

"You wanta go to jail, too?"

The cowboy said no more.

With his left hand, the lawman gave Johnny a hard shove toward the front of the Silver Bell. "March," he said.

The wages of sin. Sure, Johnny Vorhes mused, sitting on one of two iron cots in the town jail. I guess, he mused silently, that gambling is a sin. Robbing is a sin. Bedding a woman without marriage is a sin. This is what it comes down to.

The jail was a one-room building made of heavy timbers. The door was made of two thicknesses of heavy planks. No windows, no escape. His boots and everything in his pockets had been taken from him. That included his folding knife and his money. It was all the money he had. Would the hotel proprietor lock him out of his room? Would Frankie have any more to do with him?

Sitting in total darkness with his head in his hands, he refused to feel sorry for himself. He deserved this.

It was the plump Bertram Goodfellow who'd got him started in this kind of life. That was three years ago, after he'd caught a ride to Cheyenne. He'd tried to find his sister, tried to keep out of sight, and couldn't do either. He'd slept at the Dodge House and eaten at the long counter in Ford's Restaurant until he ran out of money. Then he spent two nights sleeping on a pile of lumber at the lumberyard. When he saw Bert again, he was as ragged and haggard as he was the first time they'd met.

At first, Bert tried to ignore him, but finally he took him by the arm and pulled him into an alley off Sixteenth Street. "Listen, kid, did you tell anyone about us?"

"N-nossir."

"Are you sure?"

"Yessir."

"Did anyone ask you any questions?"

"Yessir. Some men on horseback carrying a lot of guns asked me did I see anybody. I lied and said I didn't."

"All right. Here's a dollar. Keep mum."

"Yessir."

Two days later he ran into Bert on Sixteenth Street again, and again Bert pulled him into an alley. "I take it you didn't find your sister."

"Nossir."

"You have no job, no home, no nothing. Is that right?"

"Yessir."

"Mind taking a chance? I mean a chance of being arrested and locked up?"

"Well, I uh . . . I don't know."

"What I have in mind is dangerous. You could even be killed."

Their first victims were six poker players, all men of means who gathered every Friday night in a one-room house on the east edge of town. Bert and Jake wore long linen dusters. The kid wore a long yellow rain slicker. They had bill caps pulled down to their eyes and black bandanas covering the rest of their faces.

Jake went in first, crashed through the locked door like a rampaging bull, a double-barreled sixteen-gauge in his hands. Bert was right behind him, threatening everyone with a long-barreled pistol. By the time the kid came in, the six poker players were standing with their hands raised, eyes fixed on the twin bores of the shotgun. They offered no resistance, and emptied their pockets onto the table as ordered. The kid, remembering Jake's instructions, patted their pockets, chests, and legs to be sure they had no more money or weapons. Their pistols on the table ranged from a single-shot derringer to a Navy Colt. He was careful not to get between the victims and the robbers' guns. He put everything, money and all, in a burlap feed sack.

Outside, the three went in different directions, Bert carrying the sack. Johnny ran to the place where he'd left his hat. There, he shucked the slicker, the cap, and the bandana, and put on his old black hat. Back at his favorite spot in the lumberyard, he curled up on a stack of lumber, using his hat for a pillow, and tried to convince himself he wasn't a bad boy.

They were all rich, they didn't need the money, and nobody was shot. That made it all right. That's what he tried to convince himself.

It was the beginning of a new life.

Chapter Four

The sun was so bright outside that he had to hold his hand over his eyes and let the light trickle between his fingers. At that, the light was painful.

"Johnny? Are you hurt or anything?" It was Frankie.

"Took some talking to get that stuffed-shirt policeman to set bail," Bertram Goodfellow said.

Slowly, he opened his fingers wider until he could stand the light. Blinking, he made out the young woman in her long dress, standing beside the plump merchant in his dark fingerlength coat, striped wool pants, and fancy vest.

"Gaw-ud," he said. "It's darker than Old Coalie in there."

"Did they give you anything to eat?" Frankie asked.

"Naw." He exposed his face to the sun, saw it was nearly noon. "No wonder I'm hungry. How much did you have to pay, Bert, to get me out of there?"

"Two hundred. Don't worry about it."

"That policeman left me broke. Took everything off the table and took every dime I had in my pockets."

"I'm good for a loan."

Frankie took his arm. "Shall we go to Reuben's and eat?"

"Did they lock me out of my hotel room?"

"That mean Mr. Wayette put a lock on your door, but Mr. Goodfellow gave him some money and he took it off again."

"Thank God for friends."

Seated at a table in Reuben's, they ordered potato soup and sourdough bread and some butter. Johnny rubbed his face, and allowed, "I ought to go upstairs and shave. I know I look like hell. But if I don't wrap myself around some grub pretty soon, I'm gonna fall on my face." When he glanced around the room he became aware that other customers were staring at him. He grinned crookedly. "I'm a killer now. I've been playing cards in Cheyenne for almost two years, and that was the first time I ever had any quarrel with anybody. Now I'll be known as a gunfighter."

"It was bound to happen."

Frankie touched his hand. "You're lucky to be alive, Johnny. I heard that he shot twice and missed."

"Yeah. He was crazy. He pointed his gun in my general direction and jerked the trigger."

"There's no doubt how a jury will rule."

"Lord, I hope it doesn't come to that. Why would the laws even charge me with a crime?"

"Only reason I can think of is that they've got a court and a judge and a police chief and a sheriff, and they've got to have something to do."

"They've got to keep us little ol' citizens in line, huh?"

Lowering his voice, Bert said, "You know what I think of the law."

"Yeah. I wonder, uh, about the widow. He was married. I killed him and left her a widow. Know anything about her?"

"Don't worry about her. I hear she's already put the slaughterhouse and butcher shop on the market. She'll sell out and go back East and live like a queen."

"Well, I sure never wanted to shoot anybody. I hope she knows that."

"I don't think she blames you. Matter of fact, I don't think she cares a hell of a lot."

"Next problem, then, is getting my money back."

"Forget it. I'll bet a dollar to a doughnut you'll never see your money again."

"Oh?" Frankie's eyebrows went up. "How can they do that? Keep somebody else's money."

Bert was sour. "They'll find a way. They've no doubt already got it divided among the police chief, the community councilmen, and the judge."

"I'll at least try."

"You'll see."

While he soaked in a tin tub on the first floor of the Cheyenne Arms, Johnny was feeling morose. Now, at the age of twenty, he'd killed two men. First it was old Zeke Nash. Now it was Jason Bowers. It was self-defense both times, no doubt about that, but he hadn't wanted to kill anyone. He honestly believed he'd done nothing to be ashamed of. Yet he wasn't proud of himself either.

Bert was right about the money. After he'd bathed and shaved and put on clean clothes, including another white shirt with pleats down the front,

Johnny found the chief of police watching a faro game in the Brass Ass, another gaming house.

"I need to talk to you."

Police Chief Tobias Wimmer was a thick-bodied man with a walrus moustache and hard gray eyes. He always wore a white Stetson and a white shirt. His gun looked to be a .45 Smith & Wesson, and he had metal cartridges in loops on his belt. The hat was dirt-smudged. "What about?"

"The money you took off the table and off me."

Johnny was overheard by men at the table. Heads turned, and curious eyes went from him to the lawman.

"Oh, you think you can just kill a man and walk away, huh?" The lawman made sure everyone heard that.

"I'm not talking about the shooting. I'm talking about the money you took."

"That's evidence, and it's in the custody of the court." But he added, "All right, if it'll make you happy, let's go over to that table there and palaver."

Seated across from each other at a table in the corner, out of earshot of the faro game, the two men glared at each other a moment, then Johnny said, "Well?"

"Listen, you young dandy. Like I already told you, I don't like cardsharps and I don't like smart-aleck kids. Now, there's two things you're gonna have to do to get your money."

Anger was rising in Johnny, but he held it down.

"First," the lawman said, "you're gonna have to go to court and prove the money was yours, how much of it was yours. Then you're gonna have to prove you killed a man in self-defense."

"I can do that." Johnny's eyes were level with the police chief's.

"Maybe you can and maybe you can't. It's gonna cost you."

"What do you mean?"

"You gonna represent yourself in court? You gonna round up witnesses? How many witnesses do you think will go to court without bein' served a summons and ordered to go? Ever serve a summons? Any idea how much a lawyer'll charge you to do all that?"

No longer able to meet the lawman's gaze, Johnny looked down at the green felt tabletop. He'd heard this before. Something like it. Heard it from his poppa. Saw how defeated his poppa was when he'd come back from Denver and said he couldn't afford to hire a lawyer and go to court. Remembered his poppa saying, "The law was made for them that c'n pay for it." Remembered going behind the barn and cussing, using words his momma would never allow anywhere near the house.

He felt like cussing now. Instead, he swallowed hard and said, "What if I don't do anything?"

Police Chief Wimmer leaned back in his chair, a smug look on his face. "If you keep your mouth shut, keep out of trouble, don't start no ruckuses, maybe we won't charge you with a crime. Maybe we'll just call it self-defense."

"All right."

Wimmer leaned forward, put his arms on the table. "Now listen to me, boy. I'd better not hear any rumors about you bad-mouthin' me. If I hear anything like that, I'll have you back in the hoosegow so fast it'll make your head swim. And next time there won't be no bail."

He got a stake from Bertram Goodfellow and

played poker in the Silver Bell. Didn't get a decent hand all night. Went back to the hotel, where Frankie was waiting.

"Poor Johnny." She stroked his head.

But Johnny chuckled. "Poor me? What's poor about me? I don't expect to win every night? I can borrow from Bert again." He sat on the chair and pulled off his boots.

But Frankie was moody. She sat on his lap, wanting to talk. "Don't you get tired of living on luck, Johnny? I mean, you almost got killed. It could happen again. It will."

Refusing to be drawn into her mood, Johnny kissed her on the lips. Her response was weak. "Are you feeling sorry for me, Frankie?"

"Well . . . maybe yes, maybe no. You're an honest man. I believe everything you say. Most men I've known, I wouldn't believe if they swore on a whole stack of Bibles. You've never tried to fool me or feed me a line of baloney. You treated me with respect. Going to bed together was as much my idea as yours." She stood and walked listlessly around the room.

It was contagious, her mood. Now Johnny was feeling it, too. He spoke softly. "Are you maybe feeling sorry for yourself, Frankie?"

She sat on the edge of the bed and put her elbows on her knees, her chin in her hands. "Maybe I am. Sometimes I wonder where I'll end up. I mean, how long can I keep on making a living by giving men a look at my body?"

"I thought you liked what you're doing."

"Oh, I do, but . . ." A wry chuckle came from her. "It's funny, isn't it? I wanted so bad to be an actress, to perform on a stage in front of an adoring audience. I would have done anything. I . . . I did something to get my chance. Something with a man."

Not knowing what to say, Johnny said nothing.

"Oh, well." She sighed, stood, and started undressing. "Let's go to bed."

"The night won't be a complete bust."

"No. I'm having my period. I should have stayed in my own room, I guess. I just wanted to talk to somebody. Are you gonna get mad at me, Johnny?"

"There ain't nothing you can do that would make me mad at you."

Sure. As he lay on his back in the dark, he knew she was right. He was living on luck. For the hundredth time he realized that his luck couldn't last. He'd either be killed by a loser in a card game, or by the Nashes. The Nash boys hadn't given up. They'd find him.

Two jacks. Johnny tried not to show his disappointment and disgust. The short man on his left drew one card. If that player had two pairs, his chance of getting a full house with one card was one in twelve. Or, if he was trying to fill a straight on one end, he had one chance in eleven; on either end, one chance in six. If his ambition was to fill a flush, he had one chance in five. Another player drew one card. He was facing the same odds as the short man.

On Johnny's right, the call was for three cards. A pair of something. His chances of getting three of a kind were one in nine. He had one chance in five of drawing two pairs. The other man folded, grumbling, "Shit. Cain't make nothin' out of that."

It was another one of those nights. Johnny was

being conservative, betting only when he thought he had a good chance of winning, folding more often than not. The best hand he'd had was three of a kind, and somebody else had had a full house. It would take a lot of luck to make anything out of two jacks. But he called and drew three cards. Coins clinked as men tossed in their bets.

"Mr. Vorhes?"

"Well, gentlemen, I'm gonna raise you all. Let's make it ten bucks." Maybe it would work. He'd been throwing down cards all night. Maybe they believed he wouldn't raise unless he had a damned good hand. Something had to work.

It didn't. "Call."

"I'm out."

"I'll call."

Damn. He should have raised twenty dollars.

"What've you got, Vorhes?"

He was ashamed to show what he had. "Two jacks."

"Too bad. Queens full." The winner reached for the pot. "Well, gentlemen, I know what it's like to be shit on by old Lady Luck. But tonight she's makin' up for it."

"I'm through," Johnny said, pushing back his chair. He forced himself to smile. "There'll be other nights."

"Me, too."

"Hell, Vorhes, if I had that purty little blond-headed lady to shack up with, I wouldn't feel like a loser."

For a second the smile slipped, but Johnny forced it back. He didn't want any fights. "Evening, gents."

He was on his way out, still smiling like a winner, when he met Bertram Goodfellow coming in. "Johnny Vorhes, let me buy you one."

"Well, Bert, to tell the truth, I'm ready to hit the blankets."

"One won't hurt." In a lower voice he said, "Need to talk."

"Well, all right." Turning on his heels, he followed the plump merchant to a table. "What about?"

Seated, Bert leaned close. "Jake's got it figured out. He needs our help."

Chapter Five

It wouldn't do for the three men to be seen together, anytime, so they met on the west side of town in a sandy draw. Their horses stood hobbled, heads down.

"Howdy, Jake," Johnny said.

" 'Lo, Kid. Hear you plugged a man over a poker game." Jake hadn't changed, either. Still tall, thin, dark and brooding.

"Yeah. As many times as I've pointed a gun at men, that was the only time I ever pulled the trigger." It wasn't a lie. Zeke Nash's killing had been an accident.

"Bound to happen." Jake squatted on his heels and rolled a smoke. Johnny and Bert sat cross-legged. "Here's the way it is," Jake said. "The Union Pacific pays its men once a month. Two days from now is payday. What they do is, they bring the money from somewhere back East in a mail car, locked up tight in a big safe. We can't bust open

41

that safe. Not without a box of giant powder, and then we'd blow hell out of ever'thing in it."

He paused, looking at the two faces in front of him. "But the way I seen it, they move the cash from one train to the work train. That's when we have to grab it."

Bert asked, "Where do they do this?"

"Hillsdale. 'Bout twenty miles east."

"Why Hillsdale? Why not in Cheyenne?"

"The Cheyenne yards are always full. They load the work train at Hillsdale.

"What time of day do they make the switch?"

"Around ten at night. Couldn't be better."

"It will, no doubt, be well guarded."

Jake took a drag on his cigarette, blew smoke, and scowled. "No doubt about that. What we gotta do is draw their attention away for a couple seconds. I got a stick of powder, a blastin' cap, and a short fuse. When we see 'em packin' the money box from one car to another, we can light the fuse, toss it close enough to 'em that it'll make their heads ring, then get the drop on 'em."

"Can we get that close without being seen?"

"It'll be a black night, and there's some shacks over there full of railroad stuff. Yeah, I'm thinkin' we can."

Bert looked at Johnny. "What do you think?"

"You've obviously been there and looked it over, Jake. Are you sure about the place and time?"

"As sure as I can be. Which don't make it an iron-clad fact. If I'm wrong, I'm wrong."

Bert said, "If they make the switch at Cheyenne, or if the timing is wrong, we'll have to abandon the plan. But we won't have lost anything."

Johnny said, "The railroad doesn't always run on time, but like you said, we've got nothing to lose."

"That's they way I see it," Jake said.

"How do you know all this?" Johnny asked.

"I hate to admit it, but I got a job workin' on the Union Pacific once. I did it just to see where the payroll comes from and what they do with it. On payday the men line up in front of the waycar, and they get paid in cash money. I worked in the yards at Hillsdale and saw how they done it."

"Did anybody get suspicious of you?"

Grinning, Jake drawled, "Naw. I didn't even quit. I got drunk on purpose and let 'em fire me. Besides, that was over a month ago. I went back in the dark and watched 'em pack money in an iron box from one car to another. I got it figgered out now."

"Well," said Bert, "if this works, you're entitled to the lion's share. Right, Johnny."

"He's earned it," Johnny grinned. "Railroad building is hard work."

"Sure," Jake scowled, "if it works, I'm your best pal. If it don't you'll cuss at me."

Jake's scowl meant nothing. He always scowled. Johnny said, "We won't cuss at you."

"If it doesn't work," Bert said, "we'll just go on as if nothing happened." He chuckled. "Fact is, that's what we'll do if it does work."

They had little time to think about it. All that remained was to do it.

Johnny dressed as if he were going to a gaming house, but he went instead to the four-room home of Bertram Goodfellow, owner of the best haberdashery in town. There he changed clothes and saddled his bay horse, which he kept in a corral with Bert's bay horse, an animal that was broke to ride as well as to pull.

Shortly after dark, they met Jake in another draw on the east side of town. Jake was carrying a double-barreled shotgun. Bert had a long-barreled pistol. Johnny had left his two-shot .41 at Bert's house and was armed with a big Colt Dragoon, a percussion gun.

"What you want in a robbery," Jake had once said, "is a gun that's big and noisy."

The Dragoon, a pre–Civil War gun, was that. Johnny had the chambers loaded with a few grains more powder than was recommended, and when it fired, smoke and flame belched out of the bore. "If it don't hit you, it will scare hell out of you," Bert had once said with a straight face.

They cut across country, riding at a slow trot most of the time, wanting their horses to be ready to run, if necessary. Bert had to strike a match now and then to look at his pocketwatch. "If the train isn't early, we should be right on time," he said.

"Them damn trains ain't never early," Jake allowed.

They talked little. Johnny wasn't as nervous as he was the first time he'd helped pull a robbery. But he couldn't keep a small worry from tugging at his mind. He didn't want to kill again; he wouldn't. Not in a robbery. In self-defense, yeah, but not in a robbery. But what would he do if it came down to shooting or being shot? He'd thought about it, worried about it, and he just didn't know. All he knew was, he didn't want to kill an innocent man.

It gave him some satisfaction to know his partners felt the same way. They'd robbed stagecoaches and taken the bank bags and mailbags, but they'd never robbed the passengers. A Wells Fargo guard had to be clubbed upside the head with the butt of Jake's shotgun, but he wasn't hurt bad.

"I ain't robbin' no workin' stiffs," Jake had said.

"Me neither," said Johnny.

Bert put it differently. "I'm not robbing the rich to give to the poor, but I'm not robbing the poor, either."

They rode silently, hearing only hoofbeats, the creak of saddle leather, and the sound of horses clearing their nostrils. Bert thumbed a sulphur match and looked at his watch again. "We're gonna have to travel a little faster."

Lantern light showed them exactly where the railroad yard was. It was quiet. A man carrying a lantern walked alongside a big black steam engine. One of the few shacks had a lighted window. They dismounted under a small grove of trees far back from the yard. "This is the spot I picked to tie up," Jake whispered.

Working by feel, Johnny untied a burlap grain sack from the back of his saddle and wrapped it around his shoulders. "There's no train in sight," he said. "We're early."

"I picked out another spot to hide and wait, behind one of the sheds. You can't see it from here in the dark, but I can find it."

"Are we ready?"

"Yeah. I got the stick of powder with the cap and fuse in it. Let's go."

In their baggy overalls and bill caps, they walked quietly with Jake leading the way. "It's over here," he whispered. They followed him until a big, dark shape loomed before them. "This's it."

"Can we find our horses?" Johnny asked.

"Yeah," Jake said, still whispering. "Let me give you a lesson in outlawin'. Look up. See? No matter how dark it is, the sky is a shade lighter. Them trees're tall enough that we c'n see the tops in the skylight."

"What kind of a building is this, Jake?"

"A toolshed. There's nobody in it, but don't make no noise."

They waited. Bert spoke from a sitting position. "This is what outlaws have to do a lot of, waiting."

"Yeah, sometimes this is the hardest part."

Quiet. Waiting. Johnny sat on the ground and leaned back against the shed. The big pistol weighed heavily on his right hip. "She's runnin' late," Jake whispered.

Now they could hear men talking, talking in loud voices. "She ain't gonna pull outa here till mornin', but we gotta start firin' 'er up."

"She's fulla water. All she needs is a fire."

"She's a fire-eatin' sumbitch."

"The westbound'll have to be fed coal and water before she goes much further. Old Forty-nine here'll be hissin' and rarin' to go by mornin'."

Bert whispered, "That's a break for us. They won't be able to beat us to Cheyenne."

A man was shoveling coal. Another was hammering on something. The three partners waited. "Got 'er burnin'?"

"Yup. Won't take long to get 'er hot enough to boil water."

"Gotta git the steam pressure up to a hunnerd and thirty pounds."

"Tomorra's payday."

"Yup, tomorrow's the day the eagle shits."

"They gonna pay us before they head on west and pay at the end of the line?"

"They gen'ly do."

A minute passed. Then, "I think she's a-comin'," a railroader said.

"That's her."

Soon, the three partners heard it, too, a long whistle, lonesome in the night. Waited. Another long whistle, closer. "Come on," Johnny said under his breath. "Let's get this over with."

Now they could hear the chugging of the engine, the clacking of the wheels on rails. Another whistle, this one short, then another. The chugging slowed to a *whoof-whoof-whoof*. Steam hissed. A bell on the front of the engine clanged. Peering around the corner of the shed, Johnny saw the engine's lantern only a few hundred yards away. "Won't be long."

"Stay put," Jake whispered. "I'll watch and tell you when to come runnin'. Runnin' and shootin'. Make a hell of a racket."

"Maybe," Bert whispered, "we can make them think there are more of us."

Waited. Johnny's heart was beating faster. Gawd, he thought, is it worth it? Yeah. He'd thought it over before. He'd be damned if he'd work himself to death the way his folks did. Work dawn to dark and go hungry at the same time. Yeah, it was worth it. He gripped the butt of the Dragoon, got it ready to draw.

The thirty-ton locomotive *whoof-whoof-whoofed* again. More steam escaped with a loud hiss. Men were talking. The engine screeched and stopped down the track fifty feet beyond where the three partners were waiting.

"Stay put," Jake said, peering around a corner of the shed. "Get ready."

More voices. A man laughed. A man swore. Jake whispered, "They're openin' the mail car. Get ready." Johnny pulled his bill cap down to his eyes, pulled the bandana up to his eyes. He lifted the Dragoon from its holster.

Jake thumbed a match and lit the fuse in a stick of dynamite. "I'm gonna throw 'er under the mail car. Soon's she booms, run right at 'em."

Bert whispered, "Let's do it."

Chapter Six

The railroaders were caught by surprise. One man was carrying an oilcan with a long spout, preparing to oil the locomotive valves. Another was checking the wheels and running gear. Two more were lifting mail sacks from the mail car. They eased down an iron box with handles on each end and a big padlock in the middle. Two other men, armed with short-barreled shotguns, were watching everything.

Jake stepped out from behind the shed and quickly tossed the hissing stick of dynamite under the mail car. The sound caused one of the armed guards to look back and see Jake. "Hey," he yelled, leveling his shotgun. The dynamite exploded.

It sounded as if the world had blown apart. The concussion knocked down the two guards. Other men were too shocked to move. One of the guards started to get up, but found himself looking into the twin bores of Jake's shotgun. Bert and Johnny ran up, yelling, whooping, firing into the ground.

"Don't nobody move," Jake yelled. "Stay down or I'll blow your goddam heads off."

Nobody moved.

Johnny fired into the ground between the two prone guards. The Dragoon boomed like a cannon, and flame shot from the bore. The box had been dropped near two men in white shirts and bare heads. Bert fired a shot that ricocheted off the box. "Get away from it," he yelled.

A blast from Jake's sixteen-gauge knocked the lock off the box. Then Jake turned and aimed the other barrel at the two guards. Johnny holstered his gun, unwrapped the grain sack from around his shoulders, opened the box lid, and stuffed the sack with US greenbacks. He groped the inside of the box to be sure he had all the money, then hefted the bag onto his left shoulder and drew his big pistol again.

Bert fired a shot that clanged off the locomotive boiler. A man standing near the boiler jumped. With his left hand, Bert picked up the guards' shotguns. Jake took their pistols from belt holsters. "Face down," he barked. "On your bellies!"

A railroader in bib overalls and a striped cap grabbed a heavy wrench and started toward Johnny. The Dragoon boomed again, and a lead ball slammed into the ground near the man's feet. He stopped as suddenly as if he'd run into something, dropped the wrench, and raised his hands.

"Don't be a fool," Johnny said. He fired another shot into the ground for emphasis.

One of the guards got to his hands and knees in spite of Jake's shotgun. Instead of shooting, Jake brought the butt of the gun down on the back of the man's head. The guard dropped onto his face.

"All right, now," Jake yelled, "we're leavin'. Don't nobody move till we're outa sight. Make one move and you'll get a load of double-ought buckshot in the guts."

They backed away, guns leveled, Johnny carrying the grain bag on his left shoulder. Just before they faded into the dark, Bert fired a shot that ricocheted off the engine. Then he threw the guards' weapons into the darkness. They ran toward their horses.

"Can you find them, Jake?"

"Yeah, foller me."

Behind them men yelled. Three shots were fired. The bullets didn't come close. At the grove of trees, it was so dark they had to find their horses by feel. Johnny knew by the way the saddle felt that the first horse he found wasn't his. "Here, Bert," he whispered, "I think this one is yours."

"Don't matter," Jake said, "Just get on horseback. We can swap later."

Johnny untied the reins and swung into the saddle, holding the bag on the saddle in front of him. It was Bert's saddle, all right, longer in the seat than his own. But that was good. It had room for the money bag.

"Ready?" Jake said, "let's go."

Riding at a swift trot, they took a wide turn around the railroad yard and headed west and south until they came to the road to Cheyenne. "This's gotta be the road," Jake said. "Try to stay on it."

"I can't see my hand in front of my face," Bert said, "but these horses can see very well, and maybe they'll follow it."

51

They booted their mounts into a lope, believing their tracks would be impossible to discern among all the other tracks on the road. When they were a few miles from Cheyenne, they reined off the road and angled northwest, hoping to pass somewhere near a ranch house. Off to the north, they heard a dog bark. "That ranch has got to be over there," Bert said. "I hope they don't get curious about the dog barking."

"Dogs can always find somethin' to bark at," Jake said.

Satisfied that their tracks were mixing with the tracks of ranch horses and cattle, they turned in the direction they hoped was west. After a few minutes of riding at a trot, they began looking for the lights of Cheyenne.

"Maybe we're too far north," Johnny said. "Can't see a damned thing. Can't even see this horse's ears."

"If that's my horse, give him his head," Bert said. "He knows where home is. He knows where he has to go to get the load off his back."

Sure enough, the animal angled southwest. Bert said, "This one knows, too. Must be yours, Johnny."

Chuckling, Johnny said, "Hell of a note, when we don't even know which horses we're riding."

"I'm just damned glad these brutes can see in the dark," Bert said. "I sure can't."

"There's Cheyenne," Jake said. "We've got plenty of dark night left. Let's walk these horses the rest of the way and let them cool down."

The lights of Cheyenne were nothing more than dim lamp lights in a few windows. They approached from the north. At the edge of town, Jake struck out to the west, heading for his one-room shack four miles west of town. Johnny and Bert rode in a big circle on the north end, then went back to Bert's house and corral. There they offsaddled in the dark, hung the saddle blankets on a corral pole to dry, and used handfuls of hay to wipe telltale sweat off their horses' backs. Neighborhood dogs barked, but Bert said, "Those damned dogs bark all the time."

Three lamps had been left burning in Bert's house, and one was out of coal oil, burning the wick and smoking. Bert lifted the chimney and pinched that one out. Johnny dropped the burlap bag on the floor next to the kitchen table.

"Do you want to count the money now?" Bert asked.

"Not now. Jake trusts you and I trust you." He chuckled. "It's funny, ain't it? We're thieves, yet we trust each other."

Chuckling with him, Bert allowed, "They say there's honor among thieves. I guess that's right. The unwritten laws sometimes make more sense than the legislated ones."

For a brief moment, Johnny silently disagreed. There was no honor among the Nashes. He'd seen them kill one of their own gang. Quickly, he pushed the scene out of his mind. "Well, my problem right now is getting up to my hotel room without being seen."

"I'll give you your share tomorrow. I mean, later today."

"No, you keep it for a while. I've got no place to hide it in a hotel room, and I don't want it found there."

"All right. I've got a good hiding spot. We'll settle later."

Only one lamp was burning in the hotel lobby. The night clerk was sitting with his arms folded on top of his desk and his face buried in his arms. That's a soft job, Johnny thought as he tiptoed his way upstairs. He slipped inside his room and started undressing in the dark.

"Huh?" Frankie snorted, awakening suddenly.

"It's me, Frankie. Be quiet."

She whispered, "Where've you been?"

"Oh, you know, the usual places."

"I was getting worried, afraid you'd got shot."

Grinning in the dark, he said, "Not tonight."

"Well, if I hadn't've been worried, I'd've gone back to my room."

Sliding in beside her, he said, "I'm glad you didn't."

"I'm still having my period."

"Oh. Well, anyhow, I'm glad you're here."

He lay awake until almost daylight. Everything had gone right. Nobody was shot. The Union Pacific was a big corporation, and would find the money to pay its workers. No one would suffer. Yeah, it had gone right. But there was that gnawing at the back of his mind again.

Too damned right.

The news was all over town before the newspapers could get out a special edition. But the evening *Argus* was sold out soon after it hit the streets. A front-page banner headline screamed: UNION PACIFIC PAYROLL ROBBED.

A three-column subhead read: *Masked Men Overpower Railroad Crew at Hillsdale*.

Below that, another subhead in smaller type read: *"Armed Thieves Escape in the Dark of Night— Believed in Cheyenne*.

The *Argus* quoted railroaders as saying four

armed and masked men did the dirty deed. The *Rocky Mountain Star* had three robbers. The *Argus* had them all armed with shotguns. The *Star* had two shotguns and a large-caliber pistol.

Johnny Vorhes smiled when he read the newspapers while sipping whiskey in the Silver Bell. The witnesses couldn't get their stories straight. That would make it tougher on the Pinkertons, who, according to the *Argus*, had been called upon by railroad officials to investigate. Laramie County Sheriff Floyd Rathke was also investigating.

When the plump, well-dressed Bertram Goodfellow joined Johnny at a table, Johnny asked aloud, "Did you read this?"

"I heard about it and read about it. I wonder if those railroad laborers will be paid."

"I don't know. I hope so."

"Surely they will."

In a low tone Bert said, "It's close to seven thousand dollars. I'll keep Jake's forty percent until the dust settles. When do you want your share?"

"Not now. Keep it hidden."

Speaking louder, Bert said, "Well, if the sheriff sees any rough characters spending a lot of money, he'll know who to question."

"I'd like to get them in a poker game," Johnny said. He added, "I've heard of those Pinkertons. I wonder what they look like."

"They're going to find Cheyenne a lot different from Chicago."

In Johnny's room at the Cheyenne Arms, Frankie had the *Argus* spread across the bed. "Did you read this?" she asked when Johnny came in.

"Yeah. It's all over town."

"You came in awful late last night. Early this morning, I should say."

55

Studying her face, he tried to determine whether she was suspicious. Her face revealed nothing. He forced a grin. "Do you think maybe *I* did it?"

For a moment, she said nothing, but only looked blankly at him. Then she shrugged. "I'm asking no questions."

He leaned down and kissed her on the forehead. "You're a good woman, Frankie."

But, he told himself as he walked down the hall to the water closet, she's a little bit suspicious. How'd she get suspicious?

Five hours later he asked himself that question again. Only this time the suspicious one was the county sheriff, Floyd Rathke.

Chapter Seven

Johnny was sitting alone at a felt-topped table, riffling a deck of cards, hoping to draw someone into a game. Rathke dropped his wide hips into a chair opposite him. "What's the matter, Vorhes, don't nobody wanta play with you?"

Trying to sound casual, Johnny said, "Oh, I expect somebody'll come along. Somebody always does."

"Who'd you play with last night?"

The bluntness of the question caught Johnny by surprise, and he could only grunt, "Huh? Oh. Last night I played checkers with Bertram Goodfellow."

"Where?" The sheriff's gray eyes under bushy brows were boring into Johnny's face. The mouth under a gray moustache was tight.

"At his house." Johnny'd be damned if this law dog was going to scare him, and he met the sheriff's gaze.

"All night?"

"No, not all night."

"What time did you leave?"

"Why are you asking?"

"It's my business to ask questions."

"Why me?"

The bushy brows waggled. "I'm askin' ever' body."

Johnny slapped the deck of cards down on the table. "You can't ask everybody. Why me?"

"Well," the sheriff leaned back, still looking Johnny in the eye, "I'll tell you why. I've never known you to work a day, yet you've always got money, you wear dandy clothes, and you're livin' good. I get suspicious of men like you."

"There are other men like me in this town."

"I'll get around to them."

Those words were something of a relief. Johnny wasn't being singled out. But he tried not to show relief. "So you're gonna question every gambler in town?"

"Maybe. How long've you known Bertram Good-fellow?"

"About three years. Ever since I came to Cheyenne."

"How'd you get acquainted?"

"I don't have to sit here and answer your questions."

Now the sheriff looked away, seemingly studying the wall behind Johnny. "No, can't say you do. Not yet. You got a reason for not wantin' to answer?"

At least, Johnny thought, he isn't pulling that threatening lawman's authority and demanding answers or else. "I don't think anybody likes to be questioned."

"You got anything against a county sheriff trying to find out about a robbery?"

"Is that what this is about?"

"Yup, it is."

After pondering that a moment, Johnny said, "Well, we got acquainted a few days after we both hit town. I was flat broke and hungry. Bert had bought a cabin over west, and he took me in. He's a reader, and he got me interested in reading. We spent the winter reading and playing cards and checkers. Later, Bert went into the drygoods business, and I took to gambling."

"Mr. Goodfellow's got an education, I can see that. Seems like some of that rubbed off on you."

"I learned a lot from Bert. He staked me to my first poker game, and he's had to stake me a lot of times since." Johnny grinned. "So far, I've been able to pay him back."

"Where'd he get his money to go into business?"

"He brought it with him from St. Louis. He was in business there. That's all I know."

"Where'd you come from?"

"Rollinsville, down in Colorado Territory. My folks had a homestead on Wild Horse Creek. We went busted."

Sheriff Rathke's eyes weren't leaving the young man's face, but he was silent. Then he asked, "How long're you gonna try to make a livin' gambling?"

That worry at the back of Johnny's mind suddenly throbbed to life. He looked down and mumbled, "I don't know."

"How's that?"

"I just don't know." Shaking his head, the young man added, "I can't look into the future and see what's gonna happen."

Standing, the lawman said, "Well, young feller, if I was you I'd start lookin' at the future. Th' way

I heard it, a man took a couple shots at you the other night. The next man won't miss."

Johnny said nothing. He watched the sheriff walk away, a man of average height, a silver-belly flat-brim hat on his head, a Smith-&-Wesson sixgun on his hip, wide in the hips, narrow in the shoulders. He didn't look anything at all like a tough law dog.

John Vorhes was a winner that night, and happy about it for more reasons than one. Now he could flaunt some money without having to explain where it came from. He bought a new shirt at Goodfellow's Fine Clothing, and told Bert about the sheriff's questions.

"Sounds like he has no real reason to suspect us," Bert said. "But be careful."

"That business of us playing checkers most of the night is a little hard to believe."

"The weakest part of the whole plan was you not having an alibi, but I didn't think you'd be questioned."

"I wonder if all the other gamblers and loafers in town have alibis."

"Who knows? How about Frankie? Does she suspect anything?"

"I don't think so. At least, she hasn't asked me about anything. She wouldn't tell tales out of school, anyway."

Bert chuckled, "Just the same, you'd better keep on her good side."

Grinning, Johnny said, "I intend to."

Frankie was visiting with other members of her troupe in the hotel restaurant at noon. Johnny went to his room alone. There, he pulled off his boots and lay on the bed, hands under his head. He wanted to nap, but couldn't fall asleep. His mind worried over the questions Sheriff Rathke had asked, and his answers. He could find nothing wrong with his answers.

What he'd said about spending a winter with Bertram Goodfellow was true. After his first robbery, they'd stocked a two-room cabin Bert had bought about five miles west of town. Jake dropped in now and then, but he had his own cabin closer to town. Bert got Johnny interested in reading, but it was Jake who taught him to play cards. And it was Jake who taught him to shoot.

He'd brought the Dragoon over one day, handed it to Johnny, and said, "This's been a favorite gun for Injun fighters and cattlemen and settlers for a long time. You can't hide 'er up your sleeve or under your coat, but she seldom misfires and she shoots straight. Let's try 'er out."

Johnny practiced the technique of drawing and firing in one smooth motion. He adjusted the Mexican holster so the gun butt was just above where his hand usually hung. The gun was tilted slightly, with the walnut butt to the rear. He learned to put his thumb on the hammer and start pulling it back at the same instant his fingers found the grip and the trigger. He could draw, cock, and shoot the Dragoon faster than most men could draw and shoot a double-action revolver, the kind that didn't have to be cocked.

He liked firing the Dragoon. He liked the noise it made, the recoil, and the way smoke and flame shot out of the barrel. Jake once said it was the kind of gun that would kill meat and cook it at the same time. But he didn't smile when he said it. Jake never smiled.

Bert, when he wasn't reading or playing checkers, did a lot of mathematics. Using a lead pencil

61

and whatever paper he could find, he added, subtracted, multiplied. He spent as much time as he could in Herman & Rothschild's Fancy Dry Goods store, checking prices and trying not to be obvious about it. Then, one day, after returning from town, he announced that he would have to raise more money.

The three of them held up another stage between Cheyenne and Denver, but didn't get much. They held it up again a month later, and got a little more. Then, when the railroad reached Cheyenne and the Union Bank of Wyoming opened, Bert borrowed some money and went into the dry goods business himself. It was a business he'd been in before, back in St. Louis. He explained it all to his young friend.

Bertram Goodfellow had married young and worked as a clerk in a drygoods store. He saved some money, inherited some from his folks, and managed to buy an interest in the store. A few years later, he bought out his partner and was sole owner. He worked sixteen hours a day, six days a week, and the business was paying off. Then he discovered that while he was working his heart out, his wife was seeing another man, a younger, slimmer, handsome man. There was a divorce.

When he told about it, Bert's voice was so bitter he almost couldn't talk. "That damned judge," he sputtered, "gave her everything. He gave her the store, the house, the horse and buggy, everything that I'd been working for. All I got was my clothes and what few dollars I had in my pocket. It made me so damned mad that I cursed the judge and told him what kind of jackass I thought he was. He had his armed goons throw me in jail for contempt of court. I spent thirty days and nights in a filthy cell with filthy men. And all that time I cursed the judge, the law, and everyone connected with the law. I lost all respect I ever had for authority. All I wanted then was a way to hit back."

"So," young John Vorhes had said, "that's how you got on the wrong side of the law."

"Yes. With Jake's help. I met Jake in the St. Louis jail. He was the only one in the jail I could talk to. He'd been out West and talked me into going back with him. One thing led to another, and now I'm a criminal."

Young Johnny had understood. "Like my poppa said, the law is for folks that can pay for it."

"There's a lot of truth in that," Bert allowed. "Maybe some day the lawmakers will refine the law so there's justice for everyone, but that's going to take some doing. On the other hand," he added after a moment, "maybe they won't."

The two of them had a lot of time to talk that winter, and they talked. "All I know about you, Johnny, is you came from a farm in Colorado Territory and your folks are dead. Oh, yes, you said something about your father not being in perfect harmony with the law."

"It was over a dam," Johnny said, staring at the potbellied stove. Outside, a cold north wind was blowing snow and howling around the roof of the cabin. The sides of the stove were glowing from burning wood. "A cow rancher named Duran dammed Wild Horse Creek, and that ruined us."

"Wait a minute," Bert said, scooting his chair away from the heat, "back up a couple of steps, will you. Were you farming along the creek, was that it?"

"We had a homestead, a hundred and sixty acres. My folks settled on Wild Horse Creek three years before the dam, and the place was almost proved up on. It was proved up on before they died."

"I see.. Uh-huh."

"We had a big meadow where we cut hay and we had a few acres of spuds and onions and turnips and carrots. We had a milk cow and two head of beefs. We all worked, my poppa and momma and my sister Suzanne and me, but we ate pretty good and had hay left over."

"But you needed irrigation water from the creek, right?"

"Yeah. Old Man Duran never did like us bein' there. He wanted that hay meadow. So he got his hired hands to dam the creek and cause it to run further south, onto some of his land. Poppa said he couldn't do that, and he told the sheriff. The sheriff said it was a civil matter, and he couldn't do nothin'. Poppa went to Denver to talk to a lawyer about it."

"Uh-huh. I can finish the story for you. The lawyer said it would cost a lot of money to fight it in court. Is that right?"

"Yeah. Poppa found out that the side with the most money to pay lawyers would win. Or the side with the most guns. We didn't have much of anything."

"So this Mr. Duran got by with it."

"Yeah, but that wasn't all. Somebody shot our milk cow. Poppa went to the sheriff again, but the sheriff didn't do nothin'."

"That's not unusual."

"It killed poppa. He worked and worried, and couldn't grow nothin' without creek water, and one night he said his chest hurt, and next mornin' he was dead."

"What happened to your mother and sister?"

"Suzanne went to Rollinsville and got a job wor-

64

kin' in a café. She met a man named Alan Mitchell and moved to Cheyenne. I never seen this Alan Mitchell. Suzie never brought 'im home. She was ashamed for him to see how we was livin', I guess."

"And your mother?"

"She just pined away. We had the patent to our farm, but it wasn't no good without water, and Momma just pined away. She got so sickly she couldn't hardly move, and one night she told me she couldn't live much longer, and . . ." The boy's eyes filled with tears. "I . . . I buried her beside Poppa."

They were silent. Burning wood popped and crackled in the stove. The kid sniffed his nose and wiped his eyes with a shirt sleeve. Bertram Goodfellow pulled a blue polka-dot bandana from a hip pocket and blew his nose loudly.

Johnny hadn't told the rest of his story. He hadn't told about the loneliness and hunger that had driven him from the farm, about going to Rollinsville and looking for a job, about being hired by Zeke Nash and his two tough sons. It was a story he wanted to tell someone someday, but maybe not yet.

The Nash bunch batched on a homestead south of Rollinsville, but they didn't do much farming. Johnny didn't know it when he hired out to them, but they were cattle rustlers, bank robbers, and killers. He began to get suspicious when they drove a dozen calves to the farm and branded them with a running iron. Zeke Nash had joked about how, since they wore fresh brands anyway, a worked-over brand wouldn't be noticed. It was the murder that scared the kid so bad he had to leave.

The Nashes had been gone for a week. Johnny had stayed alone in their two-room shack, keeping their handful of cattle and horses from leaving the country, hoeing weeds out of a potato patch. They came back after dark one day with another man. All carried sixguns on their hips and rifles in their saddle boots. They kicked Johnny out of the house and told him to sleep in the barn. They had a big barn, twice as big as the house.

Curiosity was the kid's undoing—almost. He peeked in a window and watched the four men count money, a sack full of money. Watched them drink from a bottle of whiskey. Heard their voices getting louder. Saw Zeke Nash suddenly draw his sixgun and shoot the other man in the face.

The kid had run. He'd pounded on the door of Sheriff Walson's house, was bawled out for making a racket in the middle of the night, but got a promise from the sheriff that he'd go out to the Nash place next day and see what was going on.

Johnny had no money. He earned enough cleaning stalls at the stage and freight barn to buy a stack of pancakes—no meat or coffee. He was invited to sleep in the barn. That was where the Nash bunch found him late in the day.

"So you snitched on us," old Zeke Nash had said. Johnny knew then that Sheriff Walson was in cahoots with them. They took him back to their own barn and said they were going to hang him. They gave him a shovel and pick and ordered him to dig his own grave inside the barn beside another fresh grave. Hungry, dehydrated, he spent the rest of the day digging. Old Man Nash watched with a pistol in his hand. "Deep enough," he said, finally. "We'll hang you in the morning." Then, with a guffaw, he added, "Won't that be a fine way to start the day?"

While Johnny was experiencing it again in his mind, the potbellied stove was cooling down. Bert got up, opened the door, and shoved two sticks of wood inside. He sat, pulled his chair closer to the stove, and finally said:

"We're going to live, better, Johnny. We might not live long lives, but we, by God, are going to live better."

Chapter Eight

Sheriff Rathke asked no more questions of Johnny, but a Pinkerton detective did. He knocked on Johnny's hotel room door, and Johnny opened the door but refused to let him in. Frankie was still in bed. The detective introduced himself as Ernest Keller. He was from Chicago and looked it, in his plaid suit with a plaid vest. He wore a derby on his head and alligator shoes. A single gold tooth in the center of his lower incisors held Johnny's attention when he talked.

He was big, wide in the shoulders, with a square, smooth-shaven face. Squinty eyes kept trying to look around Johnny at the blond head barely showing from under the blankets.

"We can't talk here," Johnny said.

"How about my room, then? It's just down the hall."

"All right."

The detective's room was pretty much like Johnny's, with an iron bedstead, a chest of drawers, an armoire, and a pitcher of water and wash basin on a small table. His leather razor strop hung from a hook on the table, and a straight razor lay on the chest of drawers. Johnny declined an offer to sit in the one chair.

"That story you told Sheriff Rathke about playing checkers Thursday night? It don't hold water."

"What do you mean?" Johnny stood with his thumbs inside the waist of his wool pants.

"You know what I mean." The square face could have been carved from wood. "You play cards every night, either in the Silver Bell or the Brass Ass. But Thursday night, when the payroll was stole, you was somewhere else. Exactly where was you that night?"

"I'd tell you the same thing I told the Sheriff, but it seems you already know everything."

"I don't believe it. How about if I ask your lady friend?"

Johnny could feel his face turning warm. "You leave her alone."

"Why? You afraid she won't back your story?"

"You bother her, and you and me are gonna lock horns."

"You don't scare me. I know how you killed a man over a poker game, but you don't scare me."

"You heard what I said." With that, Johnny left the room, stomping angrily down the hall. He was angry enough that he couldn't sit still, so he stomped down the stairs and out onto Sixteenth Street. Shouldering through the pedestrian traffic, he made his way to the Silver Bell, where he ordered a shot of whiskey. Instead of downing the drink in one gulp, he sipped it, standing at the bar.

That detective was suspicious. But did he know anything? The three men who robbed the payroll were well disguised, but they couldn't hide their height. And the fact that they were disguised was a damned good indication that they were from Cheyenne and were afraid of being recognized. Johnny sipped his whiskey and worried. But damn it, Cheyenne was full of card sharps, loafers, and hardcases. Why would anybody suspect him and Bert? And Jake? Had the detective questioned Jake?

Johnny wanted to know, but he wasn't about to ride out to Jake's place and ask. The last man he wanted to be seen with was Jake.

Bert was different. He had all kinds of reasons to be seen with Bert. They were the best of friends, and he kept his saddle horse at Bert's place. Bert's horse was a buggy horse, and Bert had a buggy with yellow wheels and a canopy to drive around in. But the horse was broke to ride, too, and Bert also had a saddle. A suspicious lawman might figure that those two horses could have been used Thursday night.

According to the newspapers, the victims of the robbery didn't agree on how many robbers there were. But they did agree that there were more than two. That ought to rule out Johnny and Bert — unless somebody knew that Jake was a friend of theirs.

Aw, hell, Johnny mused, they can be suspicious, they can make all kinds of guesses, but they can't prove a damned thing.

Then another thought popped into his mind: they didn't have to prove anything. Though Cheyenne was now the official county seat of Laramie County, there was no courthouse, and there'd never been a trial. The vigilance committee had hung men without a trial. There was no prison, only a one-room jail in the middle of a vacant lot. There had been some whippings, and some men were warned to get out of town and never come back, but nobody had been kept in that jail very long. The citizens didn't believe in paying the cost of keeping men in jail.

These were the thoughts going through Johnny's mind as he stood with one boot on a brass rail and sipped his whiskey. He was deep in thought when he next saw Ernest Keller.

The burly detective walked through the open door straight up to Johnny. "Well, I ask her."

Putting his shot glass down slowly, Johnny tried to control his anger. It was hard to control. "You ask who?" He knew the answer, and his anger was beginning to boil.

"Your lady friend. The gal you sleep with. She said she don't know where you was Thursday night, but I think she's lyin'."

He talked in a loud voice, and everyone in the saloon was listening now, not moving. Johnny hit him.

He didn't think about it, just swung his right fist up from his waist. The detective staggered back a step, wiped his mouth with a coat sleeve, and grinned. "I knew you couldn't hit. You western gunnies ain't so tough. You live on the streets of Chi a while, you learn to fight."

A big hard fist came from somewhere and exploded against Johnny's left temple. His knees buckled and he had to hang onto the bar to keep from falling. Another fist banged him on the forehead. Johnny spun, turned his back to the detective, and shook his head, trying to clear his vision.

What the detective had said was true. He'd been in only a few fistfights in his life. He didn't know how to fistfight. He wished for his belly gun, but wasn't carrying it. No gun, no knife, not even a club. He had only his hands. He started to turn to his right, but a big fist whistled past his right ear. Switching directions, he turned to his left, spun as fast as he could, brought his right fist up in a roundhouse swing. He was lucky, and his fist connected with the detective's chin. The detective staggered back a few steps.

Something told Johnny to get after him, not let him recover his balance. Johnny bored in, swinging both fists as fast and hard as he could. One blow staggered the detective again.

But the wide-shouldered man covered his face with his arms and watched for an opening. Suddenly his left fist shot straight out, connecting with Johnny's nose. Now Johnny was staggering back. He tasted blood.

He wasn't aware of it, but a crowd had gathered around the two men. Bets were offered. Money was laid on the bar. Men yelled encouragement.

Ernest Keller was enjoying himself. It was obvious now that this gambler wasn't armed and didn't know how to fight with his hands. This was going to be easy . . . too easy. He wanted to make it last.

He said, "I walked in on her before she got out of bed. I seen ever'thing she's got. What a purty pair of knockers."

Johnny swung his right again. The detective easily dodged the blow. Muttering, "You goddamned son-of-a-bitch," Johnny tried to grab him in a bear hug. A knee to his crotch almost dropped him. Two quick jabs to the face had his head ringing. He was sick. He was taking a beating and he knew it.

Dancing. That's what Ernest Keller was doing. Dancing on his toes—in close and away. Every time he danced in close, his left fist shot out and connected with Johnny's face. He figured he could knock the gambler down and out any time, but he didn't want to. This was fun.

It was not only fun, it would let this damned hick town know he was no one to trifle with. When he asked questions, men had better answer. Or answer to his fists. Yeah, he didn't want John Vorhes to go down too soon. He wanted to give him a hell of a beating, make an example of him.

The betting odds were changing fast. Now it was ten-to-one on the Pinkerton man. "Come on, Vorhes, fight, God damn it."

"I'll lay twelve to one on the railroad dick."

A left fist snapped again, but this time Johnny was expecting it. This time he side-stepped away from it, took a fast step forward, hit out with his own left. Surprise. For a second, a blank look came over the detective's face. But only for a second.

Now big fists were coming Johnny's way fast and furious. He tried the other man's trick of covering his face with his arms. But then the fists were pounding him in the belly. Johnny doubled over with pain.

"Fifteen-to-one. All right, God damn it, twenty-to-one."

"Aw shit, this fight's all over."

"Naw, he's still on his feet."

Somehow, through the ringing in his ears, Johnny heard what was said. All over. He was finished.

No, by God. So he didn't know anything about fistfighting. He'd been dragged by runaway teams, kicked by mules, knocked sprawling by the hard horns of cattle, he'd had a wagon turn over on him, he'd nearly frozen in a blizzard, baked in the heat, gone hungry. No, he didn't know how to fight, but he knew how to take a beating and keep going.

Finished, hell.

The railroad detective was sucking air now. This was harder work than he'd expected. His arms were getting heavy. He had to pause a second, get his wind.

Johnny's eyes were both swollen. His opponent was only a blur. But some primal instinct told him to keep punching. He moved in, hitting, jabbing with his fingers, kicking. Now the other man tried a bear hug, hanging on. A hard boot heel peeled bark off his shin, forcing him to release his hold. Johnny's hat had been knocked off early in the fight, and he butted with his bare head, butted the man in the face. After being pummeled in the stomach, he used that tactic on the detective, felt his fists hit home.

Ernest Keller was staggering back, trying to regain his senses, but the young man followed, giving him no slack. The bare head butted him again, this time on the nose. Keller fought, both fists swinging, punching, but he was missing his target. A fist connected with his left eye, opening a cut. Blood ran down his face. What was the matter here? He couldn't let this dandy whip him. He punched.

For a moment, the two men stood toe-to-toe and

traded blows. No man could stand up under that for long.

Johnny was feeling no pain now. He was beyond pain. He swung his fists as hard as he could, felt some of his blows hit. He fought, swinging his arms like a windmill, putting as much power behind them as he could muster.

Then he realized he was hitting empty space. And then he stumbled over something, something soft. He fell onto his knees. Tried to get up, got halfway up, fell again. He was only vaguely aware of men cheering, men patting him on the back. Tried to push them away. Then realized hands were helping him up.

Standing, swaying drunkenly, trying to see, he finally made out the faces around him, some smiling, some not smiling. Looking down, he saw the detective slowly getting to his knees. Men tried to help him up, but he grumbled at them to "Leave me be."

"Let me help you, Johnny." Men had him by the arms, leading him to a table. Somebody pulled out a chair. He sat, chin on his chest, arms hanging limply at his sides, chest heaving. He felt sick. He wanted to throw up. He fought it down.

"Have a drink of whiskey, Johnny." A shot glass was passed under his nose. The strong, stinging odor cleared his head a little. Slowly, he raised his right hand, took hold of the glass, put it to his lips. The first sip was bitter. The second had a sharp bite to it. The third burned all the way to his stomach. His head cleared a little more.

"You whupped 'im, Johnny. That sumbitch's been askin' questions of ever'body and it's time somebody shut 'im up."

"He shouldn't've talked about Frankie that way. Frankie never done nothin' wrong."

"You had to fight for your woman. You whupped the sumbitch."

"Oh-oh, here comes the shurff, and he don't look happy."

Chapter Nine

Sheriff Floyd Rathke wasn't happy. He was scowling, his bushy eyebrows pulled together. He stopped first at the side of Ernest Keller and asked, "Can you get up?" The detective only grunted. Rathke then looked Johnny's way, but didn't come over immediately. Instead, he demanded of the fat, bald bartender, "What happened here?"

With a shrug, the bartender said, "They beat the shit out of each other?"

"Was any weapons used?"

"Naw. Only their bare knuckles."

"What'd they fight about? Who started it?"

"Dunno. This 'un here said somethin' about Frankie, you know, the dancer at the Soiled Dove. She's Vorhes's woman. I think he come in here to start a fight."

Rathke squatted beside the detective. "Are you hurt? Anything broken?"

"No."

"Let's get you on your feet, then." He took one arm and a bystander took the other, and they stood the detective up, held him until he was able to stand on his own. Then the sheriff walked over to Johnny's side.

"How about you, you hurt?"

Johnny mumbled, "Huh-uh."

"Who threw the first punch?

Another mumble, "I did."

"Yeah," a man in railroader's overalls said, "but he had a good reason. That sumbitch insulted his woman. That sumbitch's been actin' tough all over town, an' he finally got what was comin' to 'im."

"Is that right, Vorhes?"

"Uh-huh." Johnny forced his head up and squinted at the lawman.

"Can you walk?"

"In a minute."

"Well, you'd better . . ." Sheriff Rathke didn't finish what he'd started to say. He was interrupted by Police Chief Tobias Wimmer.

"What the hell's goin' on here? This hooligan's goin' to the hoosegow."

"Well, now, Toby," the sheriff began, "I don't think . . ." Again he was interrupted.

"This is my town, and this is my jurisdiction. If I say he's goin' to jail, he's goin' to jail."

"My jurisdiction is the whole county, Toby, but this ain't the time to argue about that. What I started to say is, they beat on each other with their fists and neither one is hurt bad."

"This one here is just a goddamned hooligan. I've had trouble with him before. He's goin' to jail. Stand up, Vorhes."

Through swollen lips, Johnny mumbled, "How

78

about him?" He nodded in the direction of the detective at the bar.

"He's a bona fide officer of the law, and he was doin' his duty."

"Sure," Johnny mumbled. "Sure, sure."

"Come on. On your feet."

"Well now, wait a minute, Toby. We can't lock up ever'body that gets in a saloon brawl. If we did, we'd have 'em stacked up in that jail like firewood."

"That other feller started it," the railroader said. "He picked a fight with Johnny, here."

"You keep out of this. This is police business."

"You know, Toby," Sheriff Rathke said, speaking slowly, "I always thought police business was ever'body's business. I'm willin' to listen to anybody that has somethin' to say. And they tell me the Pinkerton agent started this fight."

"Whatta you wanta do with 'im, then?"

"Nothin'. If they'd a used a gun or a knife, or if it was a big man pickin' on a little man, I'd think different. These two beat the hell out of each other. They're both gonna be sore for a long time."

Standing with his hands on his hips, the police chief thought it over, then said, "All right, but if he gets in any more trouble, I want the whole town to know who refused to lock 'im up."

"The town'll know. I'd bet on that." To Johnny, Sheriff Rathke said, "Your face looks like raw beef. Soon's you're able to walk, you better go someplace and lay down."

Frankie wanted to get a doctor. "There's a doctor in town. I've heard of him. Dr. Zimmerman is his name."

"Naw. I'll live."

"You sure? I'll go fetch him."

"Naw."

She soaked a towel in cold water from the pitcher, wrung it out, and spread it over Johnny's face. Johnny lay on his back on the bed. Frankie pulled his boots off and sat at his side. "What were you fighting about?"

"Aw, nothing."

"That man, that detective, he came in here without knocking. I covered up as soon as I saw who it was. Is that what the fight was all about?"

"Umph." The cool towel was soothing.

"Your shirt is all bloody. Let me get your shirt off."

"Umph."

Frankie had been having lunch with other members of her troupe when she'd seen Johnny come into the hotel lobby. Something was wrong with the way he was moving. Immediately, she had excused herself, hurried to him, and helped him up the stairs. Now she unbuttoned his shirt and got him to raise up long enough for her to slip off his shoulders and arms. She asked, "Is he hurting as bad as you are?"

"Umph."

"Sleep." She covered him with a blanket. "I'll run over to the mercantile and see if I can find some salve or something."

"Umph."

His face was too sore to shave, and he let his beard grow for three days. For a change he wore rough denim pants and a khaki cotton shirt when he went outside the hotel. He took his breakfasts and dinners at Ford's, a working man's restaurant. A few men stared at him, looked him over, but most minded their own business. Johnny realized he liked working men and liked wearing working men's clothes. It was good for a change.

Not only his face was sore; his hands were stiff, too. He apologized when he shuffled cards in the Silver Bell, but no apology was needed. Other gamblers slapped him on the back. "Ain't seen hide nor hair of that Pinkerton man since you whipped his ass," a gambler said. "Glad to get that galoot off my case."

There were two businessmen at the table, a railroader in suspender overalls, and another professional gambler. In spite of his stiff fingers, Johnny came out winner when the game broke up. He took the last pot with a pair of aces. The biggest loser was the railroader. At the bar, after the game, Johnny bought him a drink of whiskey, and when no one was looking, slipped a gold eagle into his hip pocket.

"It's a tenner," he said in a low voice. "Don't look at it yet, and don't tell anybody."

"How come, Mr. Vorhes? How come you're givin' me some money back?"

"Believe it or not, I know how it is to work yourself to a frazzle and lose it all. Take some advice and don't play cards with professional gamblers."

"You think somebody was cheatin'?"

"No. Most of the time we don't have to cheat. We know all the tricks."

"Well, I sure do thank you, Mr. Vorhes. Come payday, I'll buy you a shot of whiskey."

"Fine. But don't play cards with men that make a living playing cards."

"I'll give 'er some thinkin'."

After the railroader left, Bert came in and ordered his usual shot of whiskey, a habit he'd picked up since coming to Cheyenne. "Frankie's packing

81

them in at the theatre," he said. "Every man who comes to town hears about her act and they all have to see it."

Standing beside him at the long bar, Johnny allowed, "Her bunch was traveling from city to city till they landed here. They could stay here forever and not run out of customers."

In a lower tone, Bert said, "I heard the Pinkerton agent went back to Chicago. I heard his superiors didn't like him getting into barroom brawls and wired him to go back."

"Think the Pinkertons will send somebody else?"

"Who knows? Jake came in this morning. He bought some new Levis, and I slipped him his money. He said the sheriff was out to his place, asking questions, but he doesn't think the sheriff has any real evidence. Said he's going down to Denver for a few days. Gets lonesome out at his shack."

"It's worrisome, though. Sheriff Rathke ain't ever gonna quit asking questions."

"Yeah, but he's questioning everyone, not just us. I don't think he has any strong suspicions." Bert took a sip of his whiskey. Then, in a normal voice, he said, "Hear the Denver Pacific's laid tracks all the way to Denver now. Maybe that'll put a stop to folks coming to Cheyenne. Now Denver's gonna be the boom town."

"Think this town'll dry up?"

"No. There's more and more Texas cattle being moved up here. This is gonna be a cattle town. And it will always be an important railroad town."

"I've noticed more men in Texas hats and boots."

"This is good grazing land, and when it's time to ship cattle to market, it's a straight run from here to the packing houses in Omaha. The way I understand it, that's important to a cattleman. They say cattle always lose weight in those rail cars, and the shorter the run, the better." Bert finished his whiskey. "Well, time for this kid to hit the blankets." He left.

Frankie was weary when she came to his room. And she didn't like his whiskers. But she did want to talk. Sitting on the side of the bed with her hands in her lap, she said, "Do you ever feel, Johnny, like you want to go somewhere else and do something else?"

"Yeah, I feel that way sometimes."

"This just seems like a, oh, an artificial way of living. It ain't for real."

"Getting restless, Frankie?"

"Yeah, well, I don't know."

"Maybe your bunch will move on, go somewhere else."

"They're talking about it. They can't decide where to go."

"Will you go with them when they leave?"

"What else can I do?" She sighed and shook her head sadly. "Do you understand how I feel, Johnny?"

"Do you?"

"No, I don't think I do."

"I understand. I feel the same way sometimes. I want something different, but I don't know what."

Bert was worried when he met Johnny for supper at Reuben's Fine Foods. "Sheriff Rathke came into the store this afternoon. He sees everything."

They were seated at a table in a far corner, china coffee mugs in front of them, waiting for their meal to be served. "What did he say?"

"He saw Jake coming out of the store yesterday,

and he asked what a common working man like him was buying in a store whose clientele is the upper crust."

"Hmm."

"And he saw Jake getting aboard the southbound train this morning."

"What did you tell him?"

"Nothing. I don't know Jake. I do stock some of the new Levis, which is growing in popularity. Herman & Rothschild down the street is stocking them, too. And I said the time is coming when more of my clientele are going to be working-class."

"Sounds to me like he's just poking around, grabbing at anything."

"I wish he'd quit. He's beginning to get on my nerves."

"What we need is for something else to happen and get his mind off that payroll robbery."

"That would help."

The next morning, something did happen. The bank was robbed and a man was killed.

Chapter Ten

Johnny was up, but was standing in front of the mirror in his room, wearing only his pants, trying to shave his sore face. He had his left cheek shaved and was stropping his razor again when he heard the gunshots.

Bertram Goodfellow was unlocking the front door of his store two doors down from the bank. Frankie was asleep.

There was one shot, a pistol, from the sound of it. Thirty seconds later, another pistol shot came from the Union Bank. Then there was a volley of shots, men yelling and horses running down the street.

Johnny grabbed a shirt and ran downstairs in his bare feet. Bert turned in time to see three men wearing big hats and bandanas over their faces run from the bank, fire some shots into the front door, then mount nervous horses that were being held by another masked man. He saw the four of them spur their horses into a dead run down the street, heading west. They fired a few shots in the general direction of the pedestrians on the street. A gent in baggy wool pants hauled a long-barreled pistol from a side holster, stepped into the street, and emptied the gun at the four. The four kept going until they were out of sight.

Johnny had to push the hotel clerk out of the doorway to see what was happening. He ran out onto the plank walk, then realized he was in his bare feet and stopped.

A crowd had gathered. Ford's Restaurant had emptied. Reuben's had emptied. The saloons had emptied. Men milled about, asking one another what happened. A handful of men walked with careful, fearful steps to the bank. Two of them stood on the walk and peered inside. "Hey," one yelled back over his shoulder, "there's two men shot in here." Then they all poured into the bank.

Johnny wanted to go over, but he was barefoot and bare-chested. Bert spotted Johnny, crossed the street to him. "Did you see what happened?" Johnny asked.

"I saw them leave," Bert answered. "I couldn't do anything about it. I'm not armed, and my horse is across town."

"Did I hear somebody say someone's been shot?"

"Yep. That's what it sounded like to me. I know there was some shooting inside the bank."

"I reckon somebody went for the sheriff."

"Sheriff Rathke probably heard the gunfire himself. Yep, here he comes."

The sheriff was running up the middle of the street, holding his gun holster down with his right hand. Men stepped back and made room for him. Behind him came the chief of police, yelling for everyone to "Get back. Get out of the way. Make room for the law. Get back, there."

Johnny said, "I'm gonna get some more clothes on and go find out who was shot." He turned and went back inside the hotel. Frankie was sitting up in bed. "What happened?"

"The bank was robbed. I think somebody was shot."

"Oh, my gosh."

Dressing hastily, Johnny said, "I'll be back pretty soon."

On the street, excited men were milling around, talking loudly. Other men came running up, asking what had happened. Johnny mixed with the crowd, listening. He soon learned that the banker, Mr. Purcell, had been shot and was dead. One of the clerks had been shot, too, but was still alive. The doctor was in the bank with him. The robbers had appeared from somewhere just as Mr. Purcell opened the door from the inside and was ready to do business.

"They was the first customers," someone guffawed.

"Yeah, haw-haw, they made a—whatchacallit—a withdrawal."

Johnny didn't think it was funny.

Sheriff Rathke came out onto the walk, face pinched, and began pointing and yelling, "I want you, Joel, and you, Chester, and you and you to get your horses and rifles." He pointed out four more men, and his eyes locked onto Johnny's eyes for a second, then went past. Men ran for their homes and horses. Another yelled, "I'll go, shurff."

"Me too," yelled another.

Johnny pushed his way up close to the sheriff and asked, "Want me to ride with you, Mr. Rathke?

I've got a horse, and I can borrow a long gun." The sheriff looked at him, then looked away.

For a few seconds, Johnny was stunned. He wasn't wanted; he wasn't good enough. Men were hurrying, excited, while all he could do was stand there alone. He'd been rejected. Crestfallen, he walked toward his hotel, looking down at his polished soft leather boots. He almost walked past Bert standing in the door of his store.

Bert spoke. "I didn't hear everything, Johnny, but I saw the sheriff pass you by."

Stopping in front of him, Johnny said, "Yeah, he doesn't want the likes of me."

Bert tried to joke, "He ought to know by now that you're no bloomer-button."

The joke didn't work. Johnny shook his head sadly. "He needs real men, not a goddam tinhorn gambler."

Speaking softly, Bert said, "You're being too hard on yourself, Johnny. You volunteered. That's all you can do." They were silent a moment, then Bert asked, "Had breakfast?"

"Naw."

"Tell you what, I'll lock the store—no one's gonna buy clothes this morning anyway—and let's go over to Reuben's. I could use some coffee."

Inside the restaurant, a young waitress, with a thin face and a white apron from her throat to her shoes hurried up. "Did you hear what happened, Mr. Goodfellow?" Bert told her what he'd heard.

"Oh, that's awful. Poor Mr. Purcell. That's just simply awful!" She left without taking their orders, then remembered and came back.

While they sipped scalding hot coffee, waiting for Johnny's eggs and pancakes, Bert allowed, "You don't have to have calluses on your hands and chew tobacco to be a real man. So you don't swing a pick for a living. That sheriff didn't have to snub you that way."

Still feeling dispirited, Johnny said, "I don't blame him."

"Well, anyway, this will give him something else to think about. Maybe he'll forget about the payroll robbery."

"Yeah, there's that."

"But I liked Thom Purcell. I borrowed some money from his bank to stock my store. I still owe him some. Although—" Bert lowered his voice— "I could pay off the note in cash, if I wanted to."

"Yeah."

After breakfast, they went out onto the street and listened to the excited conversations. The sheriff had gathered a posse of heavily armed men and had ridden out of town on a high lope. There was hope that the four robbers would be caught.

A bearded man allowed, "They didn't get too much of a head start, and four horses leave tracks a blind man c'd foller."

"They headed west. It's a long ways to anywhar west."

"Bet they'll double back and head for Denver. Them railroad hands tell me Denver is a hunnerd and fifteen miles south."

"Laramie's closer."

"Hell, they're prob'ly halfway to Montana by now."

"Bet it's some a them goddam Texans. They been struttin' around here in them high-heeled boots and big spurs and six-shooters like they owned the damned town."

"Haw-haw. Texas is takin' over Wyomin' Territory without firin' a shot."

"That's what the railroad brung."

"That's what they call progress."

"Naw. I'll bet it was the Nash boys. I hear they been hittin' banks in Denver."

"Coulda been. Prob'ly got too hot for 'em in Denver."

Hearing that gave Johnny hope. Maybe the posse would catch up with them, shoot them, or hang them. But he wished he could have gone along.

He could still hear Powell Nash yelling at him in the dark: "We'll find you, Vorhes. We're gonna kill you."

The kid hadn't meant to kill Zeke Nash. It was an act of desperation. After he'd dug his grave, he'd left the pick in the ground at the bottom of the grave, one point sticking up. It was near dark, and the old man had lighted a lantern.

"All right, you young shit," Zeke Nash had growled. "Turn around and gimme your hands behind your back. You'll keep till mornin'."

He intended to tie the kid up and leave him in the barn all night, then hang him at dawn from a barn rafter. But he made a mistake; it took two hands to tie the kid. As soon as he put the lantern down, Johnny hit him. Shoved him, rather. Rammed him in the chest with a shoulder. Knocked him backward into the grave. The old man's head hit the sharp point of the pick and split like an overripe melon. The kid started to run, but heard the brothers coming. He hid behind a stack of hay at the other end of the barn.

Court Nash was the first to see his dad. He swore, and called to Powell Nash. They both swore.

"Where is that skinny sonofabitch?" Court Nash growled. "Just let me catch 'im. I'll skin 'im alive."

Johnny ran out the other end of the barn. Two gunshots followed him.

It was the dark that saved him. A moonless night. They scattered lead balls all around him, but they were shooting in the dark and they missed. The kid ran.

"We'll catch you," Powell Nash yelled in the dark. "We're gonna kill you. If it takes all night or all year or ten years, we'll find you and kill you."

Johnny believed him.

Sheriff Rathke and his posse weren't seen again until late the next day. And then they came back by rail. Wearily, they climbed down the iron steps of a passenger coach, carrying saddles and rifles. "Horses're wore out," one of them said. "Have to send somebody back after 'em in a few days."

A crowd gathered around the possemen. The sheriff was saying nothing, but some of the new deputies talked. When the word had spread through the Silver Bell that the posse was back, Johnny had joined the crowd and listened.

"Seen where they had fresh horses hid. We tried to keep up, but they changed horses twicet."

"We damn nigh rode our hosses down."

"Slept on the ground last night and took after 'em again this mornin', but they was long gone."

"Shurff's gonna send some telegraphs."

"I'm so hungry I c'd eat a whore's drawers. I'm goin' home and have my woman cook me a stack of hotcakes I cain't see over."

"Coffee's what I want. Coffee and bacon and . . . see you gents later."

Watching the crowd disperse, Johnny was feeling dejected again. The possemen had done the best they could. They'd spent two hard days and a hard night. They were volunteers, doing what they thought needed to be done. They didn't need him. Worse, they didn't catch the Nash bunch. He went back to the Silver Bell, stood at the bar, and drank a shot of whiskey in one gulp.

Then someone yelled across the room, "Hey, Vorhes. We're gettin' up a game! Come on over an' let us take your money."

"Be right there," Johnny said.

The game broke up around four A.M. Only Johnny and another professional gambler were wide awake. But Johnny's eyes were beginning to droop, and the other gambler noticed it.

"Let the rest of 'em leave, Vorhes. Let's you and me play for what we got in front of us." His name was Jonas Bark. That's what he called himself. He was dressed pretty much the same as Johnny, but he parted his dark hair in the middle and slicked it down with oil of some kind, and he had a pencil-thin moustache over a narrow mouth. He also carried a .32-caliber four-shot nickel-plated revolver in a shoulder holster.

"Naw. I'm done."

"Why not? You can sleep till noon if you want to. That pretty little blonde'll wait up for you."

Gathering his money, Johnny again declined, but Jonas Bark wasn't through. "Let's cut the cards. Winner take all. You can shuffle. Hell, if you lose, your friend at the haberdashery'll stake you again."

Johnny was being baited. That was something he'd never done, try to coax anyone into a game. Men who played cards with him didn't have to be invited. They usually invited him. There was something cheap about baiting. He had forty-two dollars on the table, and close to half of it was winnings. Jonas Bark had a few dollars less, and Johnny knew he'd only broken even. The biggest winner of the night had been a hardware drummer from Omaha.

"Naw. I've had enough for tonight."

"Scared, Vorhes? Can't trust your luck?"

The faro table had been vacated. The roulette wheel was given another spin, but no one was placing bets. The few men left in the Silver Bell were staggering drunk. The fat bartender had his elbows on the bar and his chin in his hands, wishing everyone would leave. Two of the drunks staggered over to the only occupied table and looked from Jonas Bark to Johnny.

"Whatta you say, Vorhes? Are you a gambler or not? You can shuffle."

The drunks blinked and tried to comprehend what was happening here. It sounded like two professional gamblers were about to butt heads. This was interesting.

Johnny picked up the deck and began to shuffle. While he shuffled, he watched the other man's eyes. "High card wins, is that it?"

Jonas Bark smiled. He didn't seem to care whether he won or lost. Johnny suspected then that he was the better gambler. "That's it. You can cut first or last, it don't matter to me."

"All right." He figured Jonas Bark wouldn't dare try a holdout card or a bug, not with another professional watching him. If he won, it would be on luck alone. In spite of the bluffing and calculating, luck played the most important role in gambling. A gambler had to be philosophical. You won some, you lost some. He reminded himself for the hundredth time that he didn't break his back laying rails or following a plow for this money. It was easy come, easy go. If he lost tonight, he'd win another night. He stacked the deck and slapped it down on the center of the table. He watched the other man's hands. "You first."

The small gathering of drunks were quiet, trying to hear and see everything.

Still smiling, Jonas Bark reached for the deck, picked up the top one-third, and slid the cards to his side of the table without looking to see what was on the bottom. Johnny took only three cards off the remainder of the deck. He looked at the bottom card, and knew he'd lost. The six of hearts. He'd have bet two-to-one right then that the other man had a face card. He forced a smile.

"Bet you've got a face card."

"I haven't looked, but I'll call your bet. That is, if you've got anything to bet."

"Even money?"

"You've got a little better than a fifty-fifty chance of winning, but we'll make it even money. What'll you bet?"

Johnny dug the last gold eagle out of a pants pocket, and laid it on the table. "I'll match that," Jonas Bark said, and he took a gold coin from a vest pocket. "On the count of three. You count."

Johnny counted, "One—two—three." He flipped over his six of hearts at the same time Jonas Bark flipped over his queen of hearts.

"Well, whatta you know?" Jonas Bark said. "You win ten bucks and I win forty-some-odd."

Picking up the two gold coins, Johnny watched

the other man rake in the rest of the money. He started to pocket the coins.

"Wait. We can't quit now. How about we cut again for twenty bucks?" He was still smiling.

Johnny matched his smile. "There's a lot of things I don't know, but I know when to quit. There'll be another game tomorrow night, and this will get me started." He stood. "Night, gents."

Frankie was asleep when he slipped into the hotel room. She grunted, turned onto her side, and continued sleeping. He undressed down to his shorts and crawled in beside her. He would have liked to end the night with some love-making, but he didn't disturb her.

He was at breakfast when he heard the latest news. Sheriff Rathke was seen getting aboard the westbound train, carrying a satchel. There was talk that the bank robbers had been caught in Laramie. The news gave Johnny's spirits a boost.

And it gave Bertram Goodfellow an idea for another robbery.

Chapter Eleven

"Listen," Bert said when they were seated at their favorite corner table in Reuben's, "I saw the head clerk at the Union Bank open the door, step inside, and close it again this morning, and out of curiosity I went over and knocked on the door. I had to knock three times before he unlocked it from the inside and stuck his head out. I asked if I could draw some cash out of my account, or if the bank was busted."

Bert paused while the waitress placed a platter of fried potatoes, fried eggs, and sliced bread in front of each man. Both got busy with eating, as if that was all they were interested in. "Yeah?" Johnny said.

"Well," Bert talked around a mouthful, "he said the bank would reopen in two days and no one had to worry about it going busted. He said the robbers didn't get everything."

"Uh-huh," Johnny grunted, chewing.

"So I asked if the money that was left was locked up tight in the safe, and he said it was not." Bert spread some marmalade on a slice of bread. "He said only Mr. Purcell knew the combination of the safe, and they didn't dare lock up any money in it until they could get a man from the safe company in Indiana to come here and figure out the combination."

Pretending to concentrate on his meal, Johnny asked, "So what cash they've got left ain't locked up. Maybe this clerk is taking it home with him."

"Huh-uh. He's got a wife and two kids, and he isn't about to keep money in the house. It's there in the bank, and it isn't locked up."

Johnny chewed slowly, thoughtfully. "What happens if somebody cleans out a bank? Do the folks who have money on deposit there lose it all?"

"No. These banks can always borrow from the Federal government and other banks. The Union Bank won't go out of business."

"Think we can get in there at night?"

"It's worth trying. I carried some trash out of my back door just as a clerk carried trash out of the bank's back door. The bank's door opens out instead of in, and it has a crossbar latch on the inside. It can be pried open."

"Mighty good eggs," Johnny said when he eyed the waitress coming toward them with a coffeepot.

"Yeah, but I've got to get over there and attend to business. Wish I had more time. No thanks, ma'am. I'll have to pass this round." When she left, he said, "Come over to the house around two o'clock, and we'll give it a try."

"Sure. Why not?"

It was close to two-thirty when Johnny was able to get away from the game in the Brass Ass. He was

97

winner by fourteen dollars, which, he reminded himself, was a hell of a lot more than he would have been paid for a day of hard labor.

"Figger that blond-headed gal is waitin' for you, Johnny?"

He didn't answer, just put the money in his pocket.

"If I had a woman like her waitin' fer me, I'd a quit this game long ago."

Bert's house was dark, and he opened the door in the dark, wanting his neighbors to think he was in bed. "I'm ready," he whispered. "I think I've got what we need. The trick now is to get over there without being seen."

Staying in the darkest sections of town, walking softly, they made their way to the end of Sixteenth Street, hurried across in the dark, and made their way into the alley. A quarter moon put out enough light that they could see where they were going, but just barely. Bert was carrying an iron pry bar four feet long and a handsaw.

Johnny whispered, "What's the saw for?"

"You'll see."

At the back of the bank building, they groped with their fingers for the edge of the door. Bert whispered, "We don't have to pry the door open, just enough to get this saw blade in and push up on the crossbar."

"Is there any chance the chief of police will be walking around, checking on things?"

"Him? Ha."

It took both men pushing on the pry bar to get the flattened end between the door edge and the door frame. The frame was made of six-by-sixes, and didn't give at all. But the door itself was made of two-inch planks, and the men eventually pried it open a crack.

"Maybe this is enough," Bert whispered. He pushed the thin end of the saw into the crack and began trying to move it up. "Nope, too low."

Again they pushed the pry bar between the door and frame and forced a crack between the two, this time in a higher spot. Again Bert pushed the end of the saw into the crack. Johnny helped him push up on the blade. They moved it a few inches, then met something solid.

"That's it," Bert whispered. "It's an iron bar. If we can push it up out of its brackets, we're in."

"It's gonna make a racket when it hits the floor."

"Not too much of a racket, I hope. Let's push."

They pushed. The iron bar inside moved. "We're getting there, Johnny." The bar moved again, then fell out of its brackets onto the floor with a clang. Both men flattened themselves against the outside wall and listened and watched. After a full minute, Bert asked, "Hear anything? See anything?"

"No."

"Let's get inside."

The door opened outward. Moving quickly, the two men slipped inside and pulled the door closed behind them. Standing in total darkness, Johnny asked, "Any idea where to look?"

"No. Just check all the drawers. Find your way to the front window and look to see if anyone is about. If not, I'll strike a match."

Johnny bumped into a chair, groped his way around it, found the iron railing that separated the clerks from the customers, and then found the front door. "I don't see anybody," he whispered.

A sulphur match flared. Bert made his way to the

clerks' section of the room. Johnny followed the light until he was beside Bert.

"All I know to do is open drawers," Bert whispered.

Working by feel, they opened desk drawers and groped inside. "Lots of paper, but it doesn't feel like money," Bert whispered. "They'd have it hidden somewhere," Johnny said.

"Go look out the window again, will you?"

Johnny found the window, looked out. "Nobody."

Another match flared. The big iron safe was against the far wall, with the six-inch-thick door open a crack. Bert opened it farther, struck another match, and looked inside. More papers, but still no money.

When the match burned his fingers, he dropped it. "Well, maybe this wasn't such a good idea after all. They could have taken the money home. But I would have bet anything they left it here somewhere."

"It's hidden," Johnny whispered. "Where would they hide it?"

"Your guess is as good as mine. Feel the underside of the desks."

After ten minutes of groping, Bert said, "Take another look out the window." Johnny did. "Darker than a stack of black cats out there," he said.

Again a sulphur match flared. The smell of burning sulphur filled the room. Bert whispered, "That safe is so big and heavy it'd take a team of mules to move it. They couldn't put anything behind it."

"Not under it, either, I reckon."

"Don't know. Let's have a look." Bert struck another match. "Oh-oh." The safe was standing on four short legs. Dropping the match, Bert got on his knees and reached under it. "Oh-oh," he said again. "Maybe this is it."

Johnny hurried over as fast as he could in the dark. "Find something?"

"This has got to be it. One more match and we'll know." What he had in his hand was a leather pouch, tied at the top with a drawstring. It took only a few seconds to open the pouch by the light of a match. "Yep. It's full of coins and paper money. This is it."

"Then let's get out of here."

Bert carried the pouch as they groped their way to the back door. Johnny opened the door enough to put his head outside and look up and down the alley. "All right."

Outside, Bert whispered, "Leave the pry bar and saw. I stole them from a house under construction, and they can't be traced to me."

"Put that money in your hidey hole," Johnny said. "I can't take it with me."

"Sure." As Bert walked away in the dark, he whispered, "Goodnight."

The night clerk at the Cheyenne Arms was awake when Johnny went through the lobby, but barely. There was no clock on the wall, and the clerk didn't look at his watch. He wouldn't be able to tell anyone, if asked, what time Johnny came in.

Frankie was asleep, but she woke up before he could get ready for bed. "Johnny? Late game?"

"Yeah."

She raised up on one elbow, blond hair tousled, eyes puffy with sleep. "We haven't seen much of each other lately, have we?"

"Naw. How was things at the theatre?"

"Oh, same old grind. We had a full house. I've been thinking, Johnny, I've been saving some money, and maybe I can take a trip back to Iowa for a few days. I'd like to see my folks and my two brothers."

"Maybe you ought to. You've been restless lately. The trip might do you some good. Only . . . I hope you come back."

"I will. I've been writing my folks and telling them I'm reading the Bard at the theatre. They'd die if they knew what I'm doing."

"You can travel by rail most of the way, now. Maybe all the way."

"I'm going. I'm going to ask Walter about it tomorrow. I mean, today."

"What if he won't let you go?"

"I might just go anyway."

"Then you won't come back."

"Oh. I didn't think about that." He slid into bed beside her. "Hold me, Johnny."

The Union Bank didn't open the next day. All the head clerk would say was that it was reorganizing. Some of the board members had to come from Denver, and two had to come from Chicago, but as soon as they all got together they'd appoint a new president and the bank would get back to business as usual. He didn't mention the burglary. He had to admit that no withdrawals could be made, but that was because he had no authority to permit it.

Sheriff Rathke hadn't returned, and the only one who knew where he'd gone was his wife. She wasn't telling.

Johnny slept as late as Frankie did, and they had breakfast together at Reuben's. "Let them talk," Frankie said. "They know all about us anyway."

Grinning over his coffee cup, Johnny allowed

that the troupe at the Soiled Dove Theatre had some real soiled doves among them. "Sure," Frankie said. "They switch beds like they switch dresses. At least I'm sleeping with only one man." Johnny ordered two thick roast beef sandwiches and a jug of tea, then borrowed Bertram Goodfellow's horse and buggy and took Frankie for a ride.

The bay horse traveled at a slow trot over a well-used road. The country was all green, rolling hills and tall grass. Ten miles north of town, they spotted a clump of trees off to the east, so they turned the horse and buggy in that direction. The buggy bounced over clump grass, but the seat was on springs and the ride was easy. A narrow creek cut through the willow and ash trees, and there was a grassy spot that looked to be made to order for a picnic.

Frankie unbuttoned her shoes, hiked her skirt, and pulled off her stockings. Standing in the water, she squealed like a child at play. "It's cold. Come on, Johnny, take your boots off." He followed her lead, and they hugged each other and danced in the water, splashing, laughing.

By the time they got back on dry land, her skirt was wet and his pants legs were soaked to the knees. While they sat on the ground and ate their sandwiches, he dug his fingers into the soil.

"This is good dirt," he said, showing her a handful. "A fella could grow anything here. It's like the soil along Wild Horse Creek at home."

When he thought of home, his exuberance slipped for a moment. Frankie said, "You told me about how somebody dammed the creek and caused it to change course."

"Yeah." But he refused to let the memory darken his mood, and he said, "Is that dress washable?"

"Yes."

"Then let's see who can get the wettest." Hand in hand they stepped back into the creek, stamped their bare feet, splashed, then sat in the stream and threw double handfuls of water at each other. Thoroughly wet now, they found a sunny spot to lie on the grass, breathing heavily from exertion.

"This is grand, being out of town, out here where you can see the sky. On some streets in Chicago, Johnny, the buildings are so high you have to look straight up to see the sky."

"A fella needs a little elbow room."

After a while, she stood. "I'm a mess, ain't I? I've got to get back and take a bath and fix my hair and . . . aw, I wish we could stay out here."

He sighed, "Yeah. But it might get dark before we get back."

They got back, stripped the harness off the horse, fed him, and walked to Sixteenth Street just in time to see the eastbound come in, hissing and blowing steam. Out of curiosity, they followed a crowd to the depot, where they watched Sheriff Floyd Rathke climb out of the waycar. The sheriff had two men with him, shackled together with chains.

"It's them," a bearded man said. "I recognize their hats. It's them bank robbers."

The two shackled men were not the Nash brothers.

Chapter Twelve

The news spread faster by word of mouth than the newspapers could get it out. Two of the bank robbers were in the town jail, but the other two got away. What got the prisoners caught was something they hadn't figured on. Oh, sure, the conversations in the Silver Bell went, they had it planned, with fresh horses in two places between Cheyenne and Laramie. The posse's horses couldn't begin to catch up with them. They should have gotten away easy. But what they didn't figure on was the telegraph.

Yup. As one of the possemen put it, "All Sheriff Rathke had to do was go to the telegraph office and send a message to the laws in Laramie. Them hooligans rode right into a trap. We could've saved ourselves a hard ride. Nothin' can travel as fast as the telegraph."

"Keereck," said another. "The shurff didn't even have to get on a horse to go get 'em."

"Haw. Them laws're gonna git fat and lazy now, what with the telegraphs and railroads and ever'thing."

"Yeah, but two of 'em got plumb away."

"Reckon it was the Nashes?"

"I'd bet on it."

"Did ol' Rathke get the bank's money? I got an account in that bank."

"Way I heered it, he got back purt' near ever' cent. Them two that got away was too busy savin' their asses to grab the loot."

"What's he gonna do with them two he brung back? They killed Mr. Purcell."

"Don't know. He's got 'em locked up in the jail, where it's costin' us taxpayers good money to feed 'em and all."

"We oughta hang 'em. Mr. Purcell was a nice feller."

"Shit, I c'n feed my whole family on what it costs to feed just one a them."

"Why'n hell should we have to feed 'em?"

"Wonder what ol' Rathke's gonna do with 'em."

By midnight there was more talk of a hanging, but so far it was only whiskey talk. John Vorhes lost a few dollars in a game with two businessmen and two laborers. At one-thirty, he went back to his hotel. He was going to have to get some of his money from Bertram Goodfellow's hiding place, but not tonight.

Frankie had news. "They're thinking of moving on, Johnny. They just can't decide where to go next."

"How come? You haven't milked this town dry yet."

"I know, but we're supposed to be a traveling show, and we haven't traveled for almost a year."

Just the possibility of Frankie leaving had Johnny in a depression. The depression hung over him like a dark cloud when he went alone to Reuben's for breakfast. He was relieved to see Bert there. Bert was someone to talk to.

The older man listened, then allowed, "Well, they haven't left yet. In fact, they don't have any plans at all. They're just thinking about it."

"Yeah, but if they keep thinking about it, they'll do it."

"Anyway," Bert took a sip of hot coffee, "the bank is getting most of its money back." He looked to see if anyone was within hearing distance, and said, "We don't have to feel guilty about what we took. That's only a small percentage of the bank's assets."

"I'm glad of that. Have the clerks over there said anything about the burglary?"

"Not that I've heard."

"I wonder why?"

"Probably afraid of starting a run on the bank. But that won't happen now. They'll report it to the officers of the law. It's Chief Wimmer's jurisdiction, and he couldn't investigate his own pockets. Floyd Rathke has enough on his hands with the two killers."

"He might have more than he can handle. There's talk of a hanging."

"That's his problem. No one forced him to pin on that badge. I'm just gonna go on about my business."

"Yeah." Johnny glanced around. "Which reminds me, I need some of my loot. The rent's due on my hotel room, and I've been playing cards like a greenhorn fool."

"Come over to the house tonight after I close up."

Sheriff Floyd Rathke had to carry meals to his prisoners in a bucket from Ford's Restaurant. He drew his sixgun before he opened the jail door and he ordered his prisoners to stand back against the far wall before he put the bucket inside. Carrying their toilet buckets out was a job he didn't like, but the county wouldn't hire anyone else to do it. No one envied the sheriff his job.

The talk of a hanging was getting louder in the Silver Bell and the Brass Ass. A businessman at Johnny's poker table said it wasn't the vigilance committee talking, it was the hard drinkers, the brawlers, the loudmouths.

"The committee wouldn't talk about it," a poker player said. "They'd just do it."

"This bunch is dangerous."

"Is anybody guardin' them killers?"

"Ol' Rathke ain't got nobody but hisself. If them killers had any outside help, they'd be outa there."

By midnight, the talk was serious. Johnny threw in his cards, picked up his money, and said he was going to bed.

"Already? This ain't no time to quit."

Grinning, Johnny said, "I've lost enough for one night. Maybe tomorrow night my luck will change."

But instead of going to the Cheyenne Arms, Johnny went to the jail to see what was happening. He whistled a tune as he approached the jail, in case someone was on guard.

"Who is it?"

"It's John Vorhes. Is that you, Sheriff?"

"Yeah. What're you doin' over this way?" The lawman was sitting in a chair he'd brought from somewhere and placed in front of the jail door. He had a double-barreled shotgun across his lap.

"Thought I'd warn you, there's a lot of talk about a hanging."

"I've heard."

"Haven't you got any help, Sheriff?"

"No. Go on home or to your hotel or somewhere."

"Yeah, sure. Thought I'd drop in on Bert Goodfellow and see if he needs anything. He wasn't feeling too good this morning." Johnny walked on, but he was no longer whistling.

Bert was getting ready for bed when Johnny knocked on the door. "It's me, Johnny." In his long nightshirt, Bert held a lamp close to Johnny's face before he backed out of the doorway. "Come in. Something happening?"

"I think something's about to happen. There's gonna be a mob of boozers and brawlers over at the jail pretty soon with hanging on their minds."

"It's none of our business."

"Yeah." Johnny sat at a kitchen table, put his elbows on it. "But the sheriff's over there by himself. He ain't got a chance."

"Maybe he doesn't want a chance. Maybe he doesn't care. It would be a load off his back if those two were hung."

"Yeah, but somehow I think he does care. I think he believes in the law."

"Maybe he does, but you and I sure don't owe the law anything."

"Yeah, you're right. But . . ." The young man stared at the tabletop. "I wish I had a gun, something beside this belly gun. I'm afraid to take my Dragoon. The sheriff will notice it and remember it was the kind of gun used in the payroll robbery."

"That wouldn't do at all."

"You've got a rifle, haven't you?"

"It's a Henry, a Civil War rifle. It'll shoot a round a second, but it's been known to misfire. I bought it off a railroader."

"Can I borrow it?"

"You're not going to side with the law?"

"Naw. Not unless . . . aw, I don't know. I just hate to see the sheriff have to face that mob by himself."

Shaking his head, Bert said, "One more gun won't make any difference."

"How about you?"

"Not me. Like I said, I don't owe the law anything."

"Neither do I, but . . . well . . ."

"Of course you can borrow my rifle—if that's what you want."

Standing, Johnny said, "I'm a damned fool, but I believe I'll take your gun and see if I can help."

Bert went to his bedroom, then returned with the rifle. He jacked the lever down, looked to see if there was a bullet in the chamber, then let the hammer down gently. "She's loaded. Sixteen rounds. All you have to do to get off the first shot is cock the hammer. Then she'll shoot as fast as you can lever in more rounds."

Taking the gun in his hands, Johnny looked it over, admired it. "I've seen these repeating rifles before, but this is the first one I ever got my hands on. I'd like to shoot it sometime just for fun."

"Anytime. We can go out and pop away at some tin cans. I can buy these .44 bullets anywhere. But she's got a hair trigger. Don't carry it cocked."

Moving to the door, Johnny said, "Well, Bert, I'm a fool, but I believe I'll go over to the jail and see what happens. Maybe nothing'll happen.

If I get shot, you can keep my share of every-thing."

"I'll give some to Frankie."

"Yeah. Do that. Well," Johnny opened the door, "here goes."

Chapter Thirteen

He could hear the mob coming as soon as he stepped outside Bertram Goodfellow's door. There was a mixture of laughs, grumbles, whoops, and cursing. Johnny approached the jail from the rear and stood in the dark, rifle in his hands, waiting.

A man yelled above the noise, "There ain't a goddam tree anywheres. Where we gonna hang 'em from?"

"The stage barn. We c'n hang 'em from a rafter."

"Hell, yes. That's a good spot."

Johnny could see them now, coming from Sixteenth Street, carrying lanterns. And guns. They quieted when they saw the sheriff in front of the jail. He heard Sheriff Rathke bellow, "That's far enough. Don't come any closer."

"Aw, hell, sheriff, we're just doin' our duty."

Johnny made his way around to the side of the building, but stayed out of sight.

"My duty is to protect my prisoners. You men go on about your business."

"What're you gonna do with 'em? There ain't never been a trial in this whole damned territory."

"There will be a trial. If not here, over in Dakota. If the judge here don't wanta try 'em, I'll take 'em by rail over there."

"Sure you will. Hell, they killed a man here, not in Dakota. They killed a fine upstandin' citizen."

"That has not been proven. They're entitled to a fair trial."

"You found the bank's money on 'em, didn't you?"

"The money was found with them, yes."

"That's proof enough. Step aside, Sheriff. We know what our duty is."

"I can't allow you to bother my prisoners. My sworn duty is to uphold the law, and what you're plannin' to do is not in keepin' with the law."

"You can't stop us."

"Stay back, now. Don't come any closer."

"You wouldn't shoot a law-abidin' citizen, would you?"

"You're not law-abidin'. Stay back, now."

"Shit," another voice put in, "let's just go in there and drag 'em out. This law dog can't stop us."

There were some grumbles, cursing, and still another voice. "Git out of the way, Sheriff. We ain't got nothin' agin' you, but we're gonna do what needs to be done."

"Stand back. Stand back or I'll shoot."

"He won't shoot. Let's go."

The shotgun roared. A man yelled, "Goddam. He just missed my feet. Goddamnit, Sheriff, you do that again, and I'm by God gonna do some shootin' my own self."

"I've got another load in this gun. Back off, now."

Johnny peered around the corner of the building. The sheriff was facing the mob, holding the shotgun in a firing position. A man yelled, "Spread out. Let's take 'im from all sides!"

"Stand where you are!"

"Let's take 'im!"

One man moved toward Johnny. Another moved in the opposite direction. They intended to come at the sheriff from three sides. Johnny let the man come closer, around the corner, into the dark. He cocked the hammer on the Henry. "Stop right there," he said softly.

A bearded hulk in a bill cap stopped suddenly, squinted into the dark, and saw the rifle pointed at him. "Huh? What's . . . who in the hell're you?"

"A friend of the sheriff's. Drop that gun."

"Wha . . ."

"Drop it or I'll shoot a hole in you."

A long-barreled sixgun hit the ground.

"Get out of here. Not that way, this way."

"You . . . who in hell are you?"

"Git."

The hulk hesitated a moment, then walked away in the dark, growling like an angry animal.

Looking around the corner of the building, Johnny could see the sheriff with his back to the door. A mob of about a dozen men was in front of him, and two were on his right.

"Out of the way, Sheriff. We mean business."

"So do I. I'll shoot."

"You shoot one of us, we'll shoot you. You wanta die for them killers in there?"

"You can't get more'n one of us. We'll get you."

"True," Sheriff Rathke said. "Which one wants to die first?"

"You don't wanta get kilt for 'em."

They were closing in. The sheriff was going to have to fire the other barrel. If he shot one man, the others would tear him to pieces. "Stand back, now. I mean it."

They kept coming.

Johnny stepped around the corner, yelling, "I'm on your side, Sheriff. Don't shoot me."

Floyd Rathke's head swiveled in Johnny's direction. The mob stopped and stared. Johnny leveled his rifle at the closest man. He said, "This gun holds sixteen bullets. It'll shoot a bullet a second."

Out of the corner of his mouth, Sheriff Rathke said, "Stay out of this, Vorhes."

"I'm here, Sheriff, and I'm on your side."

"It's that goddam gambler. Get outa here, Vorhes. This is none of your business."

"Whatta you care, Vorhes?"

Excitement had Johnny's heart pumping too fast, but he kept his voice under control. "I don't like the odds here."

"Shit, he won't shoot." The closest man took another step. The Henry barked. A lead slug buried itself in the ground near the man's feet. "God damn."

As fast as Johnny worked the lever, the Henry was ready to fire again. "Next time I'll aim higher."

"How many more men you got hidin' around here, Sheriff?"

"You might be surprised."

"We can take both of 'em."

Though his pulse was racing, Johnny spoke calmly. "There's gonna be one hell of a bloody mess if you do."

"We came here to do a job and we're by God gonna do it."

"How many of you are ready to die for it?" Johnny said.

"Git 'im," a man yelled.

But no one moved. For a moment no one spoke. Then Sheriff Rathke said, "All right, enough is enough. You men get on out of here. Go on back to your drinkin' or your wives, or some damned place. Just get the hell away from here."

"The vigilance committee'll take care of you."

"You're not the vigilance committee. You're nothing but a mob of hoodlums."

"Get 'em."

Johnny raised his rifle and drew a bead on the closest man. "This is a borrowed gun, and they tell me it's got a hair trigger. You can't kill me fast enough to keep me from killing this gent here."

Still no one moved. Sheriff Rathke said, "Go on, get away from here."

There was cursing and grumbling, but no one moved.

"Git."

"Aw shit, I come here to hang some killers, not to shoot a lawman."

"The vigilantes'll take care of 'em."

Slowly the men backed off, cursing. Johnny stood still and watched them. The sheriff stood still. Then they were all walking away, taking their lanterns with them. Johnny and the sheriff were in the dark.

Rathke said, "I want you to know, Vorhes, that if you'd shot one of them you'd be in trouble with the law."

Relieved, wishing his heartbeat would get back to normal, Johnny answered, "Sure, sure. I knew there was a reason I didn't like the law."

"Anyway, I, uh, appreciate your help. Why'd you

do it?" The sheriff was only a vague shape in the dark.

"Like I said, I'm a gambling man, and I didn't like the odds."

It was a winning hand. Johnny had a four-card ace-high straight showing, and his chances of drawing a ten to fill it was one in fourteen. But he'd drawn it. The best thing about this hand, though, was the possible straight flush across the table. It was that lucky drummer from Omaha who had it. Two, three, four, five of spades. The chances of drawing the six of spades were one in about twenty-five. That was the only hand that could beat him. The odds were heavily on his side.

"Raise you ten," he said, tossing a gold eagle in the pot.

Three pairs of eyes studied his face, trying to decide whether he was bluffing. "Got a straight, have you?" said a man in a bowler hat and a striped vest. "I'll call."

"Fold."

"Up to you, mister."

The drummer was looking at Johnny's eyes. That was a mistake. If he'd drawn the six of spades it wouldn't have mattered whether Johnny had his straight. He'd been lucky before, but now his luck was about to run out. Johnny knew he'd won, but he didn't show it.

"All right," the drummer said, moustache twitching, "I'll see your ten and raise you, uh, five."

This was easy. "Well, while we're at it let's make it worthwhile. See your five and raise you another ten." He glanced at the faces of the other players.

But now they weren't looking at him. They were looking behind him.

Something about their expressions sounded a warning. Johnny started to turn, to see what they were looking at. A man's voice, cold, deadly, came from behind him:

"Sit right still, mister gamblin' man."

Johnny felt the bore of a gun touch his back, right between the shoulder blades. His spine turned to ice again. His voice wavered, "What . . . what is this, a robbery?"

"No, mister gamblin' man. It's a hangin'. You spoiled our party last night, and now we're gonna hang you."

Chapter Fourteen

They couldn't do this. Not in the well-lighted Silver Bell Gaming Hall filled with armed men. This couldn't be happening. Without turning, Johnny said, "I only sided with the sheriff last night, with the law."

"You butted in where you had no business. Now you're by God gonna pay."

The smell of whiskey was on the man behind him, on his breath, on his clothes. He was drunk. His courage came from a bottle. That didn't make him less dangerous, but guessing now that he was acting alone caused the fear that had clutched Johnny's heart to subside a little. "Listen, what you were about to do last night would have been murder, pure and simple. You're not the vigilance committee."

"We're a committee, all right. We're gonna get them killers, but we're gonna get you first."

Johnny started to stand, to face the man.

"Sit right there. Don't move till I tell you to."

The faces around him were more curious than hard. This was interesting. They wanted to see how a gambler was going to get out of this jackpot. Whether he lived or died wasn't important. He was just a gambler. His death would be no loss.

"All right," Johnny said, measuring his words, "so what are you gonna do? You can't hang me here."

A burp came from behind him, and whiskey fumes came with it. "I'll tell you when to get up."

"I'm gonna get up now. I want to see who the hell you are." Slowly, holding his breath, Johnny stood, still facing the table.

"I said sit still." Johnny's blood was cold, but he slowly turned, half-expecting a heavy bullet to tear into him. He recognized the man, short, burly, bearded, in a shapeless black hat. A big pistol was aimed at the center of Johnny's chest.

"God damn it, I said don't move, and I mean what I said." His finger tightened on the trigger.

"You . . ." Johnny had to swallow. "You weren't so brave last night with a mob behind you. You wouldn't be so brave now if you didn't have that gun aimed at me."

"One more move and you're dead."

"Where's your mob? You said 'we.' You lousy?"

"Me, myself, and I. That's my mob."

"Listen," Johnny tried to smile, "why don't you just forget all this foolishness and have another shot of whiskey on me. I'll buy."

"No, you don't." The pistol bore came up higher. "I'm gonna put a ball right twixt your goddamn eyes. Say your prayers, mister gamblin' man."

Johnny could see up the bore of the gun. One

little twitch of the trigger finger and he'd die with a lead ball in the head. And this man was drunk enough and crazy enough to do it. Heart pumping, Johnny glanced again at the faces around him. There was no help. No one cared. What could he do?

The chair he'd been sitting in was between them. If he could distract the drunk's attention for a couple of seconds . . . "Listen, you said you were gonna hang me. Where? Where's your rope?"

"I'll get a rope."

"Where? Borrow it from that cowhand over there?"

For a second, the drunk's eyes moved, trying to see the cowhand. There was no cowhand.

One second, that was all. Moving fast, desperately fast, Johnny kicked the chair into the drunk's legs. In the same instant he lunged over the chair and butted the man in the face with the top of his head. The sixgun roared. It sounded like a cannon in Johnny's left ear. He got his left hand on the gun, butted the drunk again. The chair between them was knocked aside. The two men's legs were tangled in the chair legs. They went to the floor.

Somehow, the drunk landed on top, grunting, straining. Johnny hung onto the gun, knowing that if he lost his hold he would die. He bucked like a horse, kicked, twisted. Teeth bared, fighting for his life, he managed to get from under. Now he was on top, and he dropped one knee into the other's crotch.

An explosive grunt of pain came from the man. Johnny kneed him again.

Then he twisted the gun out of his hand.

* * *

Men in the Silver Bell were standing back, ready to duck behind tables, afraid the gun would fire again, and not knowing in which direction it would fire. Now they gathered in a circle around the two, saying nothing.

Johnny stood, tried to keep his knees from shaking. His left ear was numb. He cocked the pistol. "I don't know who you are, mister, but you tried to kill me. I've got a right to kill you."

Sitting on the floor, the drunk was holding his crotch with both hands, his knees together. He groaned.

"Get up," Johnny said. The numbness in his ear made his voice sound strange. The drunk only groaned, and began rocking, face twisted in pain. Looking at the gathering, Johnny asked, "Who is he?"

"Name's Younce," someone answered. "Buford Younce. Runs a work gang over at the round-house."

"He ain't a bad feller to work for," another said. "But he goes a little crazy when he's drinkin'."

"A man like that," Johnny said, "has no business with this." He looked down at the hogleg pistol in his hand, and wished his ear would get back to normal.

"You're right, he oughtn't be packin' iron when he's drinkin'."

"Are any of you a friend of his?" Some hearing was returning to his left ear now, but it was a ringing sound.

"I work for 'im."

Johnny let the hammer down on the gun. "Here. Give him this tomorrow. Not tonight, tomorrow."

"I'll do 'er."

"Remind him that I could have killed him."

"I'll do that, too."

Turning back to the table, Johnny picked up his money, and eyed the pot in the middle. "We didn't get to finish this hand," he said. "I trust nobody has touched anything."

"Naw, but you win," the Omaha drummer said. "I was about to fold."

Johnny scooped up the pot and stuffed it into his coat pockets.

"Since I paid for it, I'd like to see what you got," the drummer said. The hole card was flipped over. "You wasn't bluffin', was you?"

A small smile turned up one corner of Johnny's mouth. "Not this time. Tomorrow night, who knows?"

"Wanta play some more?"

"Naw. I've had about all the excitement I can stand for one night."

"You gonna give us a chance to win our money back?"

"Tomorrow night. I'll be here. That's a promise. Hell," Johnny grinned, "I'm here every night."

Frankie wasn't in his room at the Cheyenne Arms, but before he could get his shirt off, she was knocking softly on the door. She was wearing her long robe buttoned to her throat, and fuzzy rabbit fur slippers on her feet. Johnny didn't want to tell her about his brush with death, but he knew she'd hear about it sooner or later and she'd demand to know why he hadn't mentioned it. So he told her.

"Oh, my." She sat on the edge of the bed, worry wrinkles between her eyes. "My, oh, my. That's twice now somebody has tried to kill you. And I heard about what happened last night, too. Why didn't you tell me? One of these nights you won't be so lucky and they'll carry you out of that saloon on a plank."

Trying to make a joke of it, Johnny grinned, "I didn't come out of there without hurting a little. My left ear is ringing like a church bell."

"How come?"

"A gun went off close to my ear."

"You're lucky it missed. What's the man's name?"

"Younce. Buford Younce. He's a boss of some kind at the roundhouse." He sat on the bed beside her.

"Younce. That's almost like my name."

"You told me your last name once, it's, uh, let's see, Youree."

"Yes, but don't change the subject. I'm not through scolding you for taking so many chances."

Smiling mischievously, he tousled her blond hair. "What've you got on under that robe?"

"None of your business." He started to unbutton the top. She grabbed his hand. "I'll tell you when you can do that."

Laughing, he pushed her onto her back. "Oh yeah? Wanta rassle?"

Giggling, she said, "Just because you're bigger than me . . ." She squirmed.

"I'm bigger, but you're slicker. You're like trying to grab hold of a live fish."

Laughing, giggling, they rolled on the bed. He managed to get two more buttons undone, and he could have pulled the robe off her shoulders, but he didn't. "Hold still a minute. Give a fella a chance."

"I'll give you a good scratching, that's what I'll give you." She rolled on top of him, laughing.

"Hey, wait a minute. Wait just a minute, now. I wanta ask you something."

"What?"

"You said once your real first name is Frances. What's your middle name?"

Sitting astraddle him, hair in her face, robe above her knees, she said, "Katherine. So what?"

"Frances Katherine Youree."

"Don't say it, Johnny. Don't you dare say it."

"Well," he laughed, "you could shorten Youree to You."

"I'm warning you, Johnny, don't you say it."

"Say what?"

"I know what you're thinking."

Still laughing, he said, "Well, if your name is Frances Katherine You, and your initials are F.K., uh . . ."

"Oh, ain't you smart. You're not the first one to think of that, Mr. smart-aleck Johnny Vorhes."

"Well . . ." He was laughing so hard he couldn't finish what he'd started to say.

Her fingernails were against his cheek now, but she was smiling. "You're gonna look funny going around with your face all scratched up."

"All right, all right, I won't say it."

"Promise?"

"I promise."

"Uh," he grunted, no longer laughing, "mind if I call you Frances?"

"I wish you would. I wish everybody would."

"Then why . . . ?"

"They call me what they want, and there ain't much I can do about it."

"No, I guess, being a girl, there ain't. I'll call you Frances from now on."

She rolled off him and lay on her side, facing him. "Johnny, could we go for a picnic again? I like getting out away from town."

"Sure, Frances. If it doesn't rain, we can go tomorrow."

It didn't rain. The Wyoming sky was a clear blue. The sun was high overhead. There was no wind. Even the horse seemed to be glad to get out of his pen and go someplace. He trotted right along and kept the buggy wheels humming. Johnny had folded the canvas top down and put the bag of sandwiches behind the spring seat, along with the borrowed Henry rifle.

When she saw the rifle, Frankie had asked, "Why the gun?"

"I thought it might be fun to shoot at a target. This gun is supposed to shoot a bullet a second, and I'd like to try it out."

"Don't shoot it, Johnny. I don't like guns. I'm scared of guns."

"Well, all right."

Stretching her arms straight up, Frankie said, "O-o-h, it's grand. What a beautiful day!"

"Sure is. What say, shall we go to the same spot?"

"Let's. You can tell the horse to slow down. We're in no hurry."

Johnny pulled back on the driving lines a little, and the horse slowed to a shuffling trot.

"Do you like to sing, Johnny?"

"I used to. If you sing, don't make the wrong kind of sounds."

Laughing, she said, "When I was a little girl I thought it was funny to sing something like *O-o-h Susannah*, and the horses thought I said *Whoa*."

126

Sure enough, the horse stopped. "Now look what you've done," Johnny laughed. "Geeyup, there."

At their picnic spot among the willow and maple trees, they splashed in the water, rolled on the grass, then lay on their backs and looked at the sky. When the flies became bothersome, Frankie flipped her long skirt over her face, and Johnny covered his face with his hat. Finally, she stood. "Time to get back to the grindstone. I wish . . ."

Sitting, pulling on his boots, Johnny asked, "You wish what?"

"Oh, I don't know. I wish something. I don't know what."

They got the horse and buggy headed back toward the road, the buggy riding rough over the bunch grass. Frankie was humming a tune. Johnny was just smiling, enjoying himself. But suddenly his smile vanished.

"Uh-oh."

"What? What is it?"

"Over there." He pointed east at six horsemen riding toward them out of a swale.

"Who are they? Oh my gosh, are they Indians?"

"Must be Sioux."

"Are they friendly?"

"They tell me there ain't any friendly Sioux."

"Oh, my gosh, they're coming. They're coming on a run."

"Can you drive this horse, Frances?"

"Sure."

He handed her the driving lines, crawled back of the seat, and picked up the Henry rifle. "They ain't friendly, that's for sure. They've got long guns. Here they come. Goose that horse, Frances."

Frankie yelled, "Heeyup, there. Heeyup." The

horse leaned into its collar and got into a trot, then into a gallop. The buggy bounced over the bunch grass. Frankie yelled and flipped the end of a driving line at the horse's rump.

"Heeyup. Heeyup, there."

Chapter Fifteen

The Indians fired first. Johnny heard the slug zing past his head and saw the puff of smoke. He knelt on one knee and fired the Henry, but the bouncing buggy spoiled his aim. Two more shots came from the Indians. They were riding right at the buggy, war-whooping, shooting. But their aim from the backs of running horses wasn't accurate, either.

But—Johnny gulped when he thought about it— they didn't have to hit the humans, only the horse. The horse was a big target. One bullet would stop it. Then the man and woman in the buggy would be easy game.

Goddam. He gritted his teeth with frustration. If only he could hold the Henry's sights steady for a second. He fired again. Missed again.

The buggy bounced. Frankie yelled at the horse, *"Heeyup. Heeyup."* The horse couldn't run at full speed pulling the buggy. The Indians were gaining.

Johnny tried rapid fire—three shots in three seconds. More bullets zinged around him. A slug tore into the wooden seat only inches from where Frankie was sitting.

Damn it, damn it, damn it. If they got any closer, they wouldn't miss.

Then the horse and buggy reached the road, and the buggy bounced less. A painted Indian on a gray horse raced alongside, only about fifty feet to the east, and pointed a long-barreled pistol at Johnny. Johnny aimed and fired hastily, and thought for a second he'd missed. But the Indian suddenly dropped his pistol, clutched his shoulder, and fell onto the horse's neck, and from there to the ground.

The buggy horse was running its best, Frankie yelling and pleading. Another bullet slammed into the seat. Johnny took aim at a buck with long black hair streaming behind him, squeezed the trigger. The Indian's horse staggered, then turned a somersalt, pitching the Indian over its head. "Goddam," Johnny muttered. He fired three more shots in three seconds.

Then it was over. The Indians reined up.

Still yelling at the buggy horse, still trying to urge more speed out of it, Frankie looked over her shoulder and saw the Indians were no longer chasing them. "What happened?"

"I think they've had enough. You can slow this horse down now. We don't want to run Bert's horse to death."

"Whoa. Whoa, now." Frankie pulled back on the lines, got the horse slowed to a trot, then a walk. The animal was blowing hard through flared nostrils. Its sides were heaving. "Let him walk till he cools down," Johnny said.

"Why did they give up?"

"I think the price was too high. I shot one off his horse and I shot the horse from under another one. I wished I'd aimed higher."

"Why didn't they shoot our horse? They were close enough."

"I'd guess," Johnny said, thoughtfully, "that our horse is what they wanted. Indians can't get enough horses. Yeah, that's probably it. They wanted to kill us and take the horse."

"Instead they lost a horse."

"They lost a horse and they lost a man. And when they saw how fast this Henry can shoot, they figured they'd better just give it up."

"Boy, oh, boy, Johnny, this ain't the way to end a perfect day."

"No," Johnny grinned, "but this will give you something to write home about."

Bert Goodfellow's bay horse was still excited and nervous when they "whoaed" at his corral. Johnny unhitched the horse from the singletree, stripped the harness off, and led it in a big circle until it quieted. Frankie went on to the hotel to take a bath and get ready for her night's work. In the lobby, she met two members of her troupe, and told them about the Indians. By the time Johnny got back to the hotel, the news had spread.

"Six of 'em, you say?" asked a black bearded man in a dirty cotton shirt and a round-brim hat. "Sioux, I'll bet."

"Yeah, had to've been Sioux. It's gettin' too hot for 'em over in Dakota, and they prob'ly drifted over here, lookin' for scalps."

"Scalps is what they're after, sure 'nuff. Scalps and hosses. They ain't hungry, what with all the antelope around here."

131

"We oughta git after 'em. We cain't have 'em threatenin' folks in this territory."

"They're long gone by now."

"What kinda guns they got, Vorhes?"

"I didn't get a good look at them, but I did see one buck open a trap door on his to reload."

"Army carbines, I'll bet. I heered the Warshington gover'ment was givin' 'em guns to hunt with."

"Haw. The only animals they hunt are white folks and white folks' cattle."

"The onliest thing them jackasses in Warshington know about Injuns is what them panty-waist crybabies are a-tellin' 'em."

"I had to bury a neighbor and his wife and two young'uns that was butchered by the 'Rapahoe in Colorada. I wish some of them tear-jerkers that're cryin' 'bout the poor mistreated Injuns'd been there."

The men's water closet in the Cheyenne Arms was a busy place, and Johnny had to wait his turn for a bath. By then the water was cold, but he'd taken cold baths before. He dressed completely before he left the room and went to his own room. Women could walk down the hall in their bathrobes, but men weren't seen that way.

The scars from the fistfight with Ernest Keller had healed, he noticed with satisfaction. But, he thought when he grimaced at himself in the mirror, he wished he hadn't chipped that front tooth. The grimace turned to a wry grin when he remembered how it had happened.

He was hauling hay from the big meadow across the creek in a horse-drawn wagon with no seat. He'd had to stand in the wagon right behind the team. The horses swerved just as they were going through a gate. A front wagon wheel hit the gate-post. Young Johnny Vorhes was thrown out of the wagon head-first, right under the hind feet of the horses.

"Huh," he snorted, remembering. If that detective thought he was handing out punishment, he should have been where Johnny was then.

He never did know whether one of the two horses had kicked him in the face or whether he'd just landed on his face. He was barely conscious enough to drag himself out from under the doubletree. If the wagon wheel hadn't been lodged tight, the wagon would have been pulled over him, and he'd probably have been crushed to death. The horses had quieted and stood still while he lay on his back and wished the sky would stop spinning. When finally he did get back to the barn, he unloaded the wagon, unhitched the team, and walked on unsteady feet to the house. Only Suzanne was in the house at the time, and she was horrified.

Clucking like a mother hen, she said, "You look like you put your face in the meat grinder, Johnny. Sit down here and let me wash the blood off." His older sister had nursed him as if he were her child. The loose tooth had them both worried, but Suzanne fixed him some potato soup so he wouldn't have to put any pressure on the tooth, and eventually the roots strengthened again. But the chip would always be there—unless he could pay for a gold filling. Well, he could pay now, that is, if he could find a dentist who knew how to do that kind of work. But maybe he didn't want a gold filling. Gold fillings looked worse than chipped teeth.

Ernest Keller had had a gold filling. Johnny wondered whether he'd knocked it loose. Grinning, grimacing, he hoped so.

But the grin vanished when he again remembered Suzanne. Sweet, gentle Suzanne. He was her baby brother, and there was nothing she wouldn't do for him.

Oh, God—a lump formed in his throat—he wished he could find her.

The hardware drummer from Omaha insisted on seven-card draw, which wasn't Johnny's favorite game. The odds were entirely different in seven-card poker. He was outvoted. Two of the other three gents at the table wanted to play seven-card, so Johnny agreed. His first hand was three of a kind, but that wouldn't win in this game. Hell, a full house probably wouldn't win. He drew four cards, but didn't improve his hand, so he folded.

The ante was a dollar, and when the cards were dealt again, more money was tossed onto the center of the table. Another three of a kind. He tried to figure out in his head what his chances were of making something out of it. If he drew four cards again . . . hell, it was anybody's guess. He raised the bet three dollars. Everyone called. Sure. Why not? Anything was possible.

"I'll take four," Johnny said. He didn't even look at his hand until all the cards were dealt and the drummer had bet two dollars. This gent usually bet more than two dollars when he had a good hand. He was no threat. But Jonas Bark, sitting on his left, raised him two dollars. Now was the time to look.

Four nines. A damned good hand in five-card draw, but in a seven-card game? Well, hell, he'd come here to gamble. Johnny raised five dollars. The drummer had once made the mistake of thinking Johnny was bluffing, and he didn't make that mistake again. Another man folded, too. A third player raised a dollar. He's got a good hand, but he's not sure of himself, Johnny thought. But the gambler on Johnny's left saw that and raised another five.

More cards went face-down. That left Johnny and Jonas Bark. The slick-haired gambler grinned at Johnny. "Well, Vorhes, whatta you say?"

It wasn't the possibility of losing that had Johnny's stomach turning sour. He expected to lose now and then. It was the possibility of losing to Jonas Bark—again. He forced a drawl into his voice. "Last I heard, this was a gambling game. Make it five more."

"Well, now," Jonas Bark said, "this could go on all night. There's more hands to be dealt. See you."

Johnny's face didn't change expression, but inwardly he laughed. This was probably the biggest pot of the night, and it was his. He would have bet that his opponent had a full house. They both turned their cards over.

Yep. Aces full. But Jonas Bark's smile didn't slip as Johnny raked in the pot. He said, "It's your deal, Vorhes."

Frankie was waiting when he went to his room. She was fully dressed, sitting in the chair with her hands folded in her lap. Johnny sensed that she had something on her mind.

She said simply, "I'm going home, Johnny."

"You . . . you're coming back, ain't you?" His breath caught in his throat as he waited for her answer.

"I don't know. I think so. I'm just homesick, I

guess. I haven't seen my folks for almost two years, and I'm kinda worried."

Sitting on the bed, facing her, Johnny asked, "What are you worried about, Frances?"

She sighed. "I'm afraid my youngest brother might decide to come west to see what there is to see. Traveling is easy now. I don't want him to see what I'm doing."

"Oh." Johnny nodded. "I, uh, personally don't think you're doing anything so bad, but I guess I know what you mean."

They were silent a moment. Johnny felt an emptiness in his chest. Then he asked, "What did your boss say?"

"He doesn't like it, but he didn't fire me. He said he might take me back and he might not."

"I'm betting he will. You're the main draw in his show."

"He said he's gonna take the show somewhere else, maybe Denver."

"Yeah. I hear Denver's booming now."

"How long do you think you'll stay here, Johnny?"

"I don't know. I've been thinking of taking a trip to Denver myself. I'll try again to find my sister. Maybe I'll get lucky this time."

"I hope you find her, Johnny. I know how much she means to you."

"Yeah."

Suddenly, Frankie stood, took a long step to the bed and sat beside him. "Hold me, Johnny."

Sheriff Rathke didn't have to worry about his prisoners another night. Two U.S. marshals showed up at his house and announced that they were taking the prisoners to Dakota for trial. They'd conducted trials there before, and they had a prosecutor. The marshals didn't know yet which witnesses the prosecutor would need. They'd keep in touch by telegraph.

A small crowd gathered at the Union Pacific depot to see the marshals and their shackled prisoners off. Also on that train was Frances Katherine Youree.

"If you leave Cheyenne, Johnny, leave a message with Mr. Goodfellow at the dry goods store or the clerk at the hotel so I'll know where to find you."

Johnny tried to sound nonchalant, but he had to swallow a lump in his throat. "Sure. You betcha."

"Is that a promise?"

"Ironclad."

Walking back to his hotel, he felt hollow inside. He tried to give his morale a boost by dropping in on Bertram Goodfellow.

"She's gone, huh?"

"Yeah."

"Expect her back?"

"I don't know. She doesn't know."

"The experiences I've had with women don't make me an expert. I can't figure them out. But anyway, I'm glad you stopped in. I, uh . . ." Bert glanced around the big room full of racks of clothes, and lowered his voice. "I got a telegraph from Jake. He's at the Goldfield Hotel on Holliday Street, and he wants to see us. I can't go. I can't leave the store that long. But maybe the two of you can do whatever he has in mind to do."

"I was planning on going down to Denver anyway." A wry grin touched Johnny's face. "Who knows, maybe whatever scheme Jake has is what I need."

"It'll take your mind off everything else. But be careful, plan carefully."

The wry grin widened. "You know I'd never do anything dangerous."

Chapter Sixteen

The last time Johnny had traveled to Denver he'd taken a stage from Evans where the railroad had ended. Now, the train stopped at Evans only long enough to take on coal and water, then went on south. While it was there, Johnny noticed a new wood frame house east of the tracks, near a big barn. The one-story house had been built of lumber hauled by rail. It wasn't far from Evans east to Rollinsville, or from Rollinsville to the Nash homestead.

Thinking of the Nashes suddenly brought a realization to Johnny: the name no longer struck fear in his guts. Instead, it was irritating. Well, he said to himself, at age twenty, it's about time I grew up.

The railroads had made life better for everyone who lived anywhere near them. But the rail cars didn't ride any easier than a horse-drawn coach. Instead of bouncing passengers up and down, the rail coach rocked passengers from side to side. On the west, the Front Range of the Rocky Mountains rose steeply into a jagged skyline. On the east, the country was mostly prairie. Pulling up a window to get some air, Johnny got a cinder in his eye. Heavy black smoke blew from the engine back through the window.

"Mister, would you please be so kind as to shut that window?" The woman wore a long gray dress, a poke bonnet, and a stern expression.

"I beg your pardon, ma'am." Johnny pulled the window down. He tried not to bump shoulders with the woman beside him on the wooden, straight-backed seat, but the swaying car made that impossible. Anyhow, she bumped him as much as he bumped her.

"The best thing about a rail car," Johnny said, trying to make conversation, "is you can stand up and walk up and down the aisle. Stretch your, uh, lower limbs."

"Humph."

"Well, if I may, ma'am, I would like to get up and do that."

Reluctantly, the woman scooted as far back in her seat as she could and moved her knees to one side so he could squeeze by. When he returned, he offered to change seats with her, but she said she believed she'd stay where she was, thank you.

"I hear," Johnny said, trying again to make conversation, "that another railroad will soon reach Denver from the east."

"For your information, sir, the Kansas Pacific has already reached Denver." The way she said it gave him to understand that she was through talking.

"Oh." He didn't much want to talk to her anyway.

It took eight hours to travel from Cheyenne to

Denver, what with stops for coal and water, and the passengers were all relieved when the big engine finally chugged into the Denver yards. They passed stock pens filled with longhorn cattle, soon to be loaded on rail cars and shipped to the packing houses back East. There were long, low warehouses with spur tracks in front. Stockcars, boxcars, and gondolas loaded with coal were parked on the side tracks.

Carrying two carpetbags with leather handles, Johnny walked up Seventeenth Street to Holliday Street. On the corner, he set the satchels down and looked at his surroundings. Denver was growing fast, now that the railroads had arrived, and the log cabins he'd seen before were rapidly being replaced by two-story brick buildings. It had been raining in Denver, and the streets were ankle-deep in mud. Horse-drawn vehicles of all kinds crowded the streets. Pedestrians of all kinds crowded the plank walks.

Holliday Street appeared to have become the bowery of Denver, a street of cheap saloons, bawdy houses, and cafés with fly-specked windows. If Jake had a robbery in mind, Johnny didn't want to be seen with him any more than he had to. So, he'd find another hotel. He picked up his bags, waded through the mud at the intersection, and went on up Seventeenth to Larimer Street. There he rented a room on the second floor of the Great Northern Hotel, a brick building with a carpeted lobby, a half-dozen wooden chairs, and a mahogany registration desk.

His room was about the same caliber as his room at the Cheyenne Arms, except that there was only one window. The window was so close to the brick building next door that very little, if any, breeze came through. Though the sky was cloudy, the room was stifling.

"Aw," Johnny grumbled to himself, "a damned tent would be better than this." He unpacked his satchels, but left the two-shot belly gun and the Colt Dragoon in the bottom of one. His powder flask and box of lead balls and percussion caps had been packed carefully beside the guns. He'd noticed that few men in Denver had weapons in view. But he would have bet that there were plenty of pistols under their coats. He'd go unarmed for the time being.

He washed his face out of a china basin, straightened his fingerlength coat, vest, and wool pants the best he could, put on his homburg, and went looking for a meal and Jake.

A restaurant on the corner of Larimer and Sixteenth streets served him a fair-to-middlin' steak for seventy-five cents. With that under his belt, he tried to figure out where he was most likely to bump into Jake. Not at Jake's hotel, the Goldfield. He sure didn't want to ask at the registration desk for him. Where, then?

Johnny walked three blocks on Larimer Street, peering in the windows of the eating houses, stepping into the saloons long enough to see that Jake wasn't there. Next he went to Holliday Street and did the same. Some of the saloons smelled of stale beer, cheap wine, and urine. Women overloaded with makeup and cheap perfume grinned invitations at him. After Frankie, they looked like pigs. He stepped inside the Gold Rush Gaming Emporium and saw Jake.

The place was crowded with slouchy men in dirty, baggy clothes. Jake was standing at a scarred bar made of pine wood. He had one foot on a brass rail between two brass spittoons. He wore baggy overalls and a bill cap, and he had a beard. There were poker tables, a roulette wheel, and a faro table. Behind the faro table an amateurish painting of a striped tiger hung on the wall. "Step up here, gentlemen," the faro dealer was saying. "Try your luck at bucking the tiger. Step right up."

Johnny felt out of place in his long coat, wool pants, and homburg, but no one paid him any attention. He sidled up to the bar next to Jake, but said nothing. Jake recognized him, but pretended he didn't.

"Whatta you want, mister?" a thick-bodied bartender asked.

"Whiskey, no chaser. Bourbon."

"Bourbon costs more, but . . ." The bartender looked Johnny over. "I reckon you can pay for it."

"How much for a shot of good Kentucky bourbon?"

"A buck a shot."

"Fair enough."

Without looking his way, Jake said, "The rotgut they sell in here's only two-bits."

Grinning, Johnny said, "I've got more respect for my guts."

The dark, sour-faced Jake looked him over now, from the muddy boots made of fine calfskin to the homburg. "Yeah, I reckon you would. Where yuh from, mister?"

"I just came down from Cheyenne. This is the first time I've been in Denver in two years. It doesn't look the same."

"It ain't the same. This used to be a respectable street."

"Yeah, I, uh, I guess I wandered into the wrong place."

A shot of whiskey and a glass of water for a chaser was set in front of him. "Pay now."

Johnny paid.

The Gold Rush Gaming Emporium was so noisy it wasn't necessary to whisper. Jake asked, "Bert here?"

"No. He couldn't make it."

"See yuh at nine o'clock in the mornin' in front of the Planter's House at Sixteenth and Blake. There's always so many people there we won't be noticed."

"All right. What's your plan?"

"Cain't say much here, but see that faro table over yonder? It's a brace game. I been watchin'. The dealer's playin' both ends against the middle. He can deal from the bottom or the top or in between. He's rich."

"I get it."

"See yuh in the mornin'." Jake backed away from the bar, turned, and left.

Sipping his whiskey, Johnny watched the faro game from his spot at the bar. He never liked the game himself. It took too little skill. Sure, a player could watch the abacus-like case, and keep track of which cards had been played. But there was no bluffing, no counting odds, no trying to outthink the other players. It was more luck than anything else.

The dealer-banker, a thin man with thick, curly hair growing low on his forehead, called out in a singsong voice, "All rightee. A winner here. A king wins. There's still room at the table, gentlemen. Step up and buck the tiger!" Out of curiosity, Johnny went over for a closer look. "From your appearance, sir, I'd say you're a gambling man. Care to try your luck?"

Johnny ignored him, only watched. The table

144

was imprinted with two rows of cards, all spades. Bettors put their chips on an imprint, and when all bets were placed the dealer drew a card from a box. The first card drawn was the loser. All chips on the corresponding imprint lost, and the chips went into the dealer's bank. The second card drawn was the winner, and the dealer matched the chips placed on that imprint. Chips on the other imprints neither won nor lost.

After watching a few minutes, Johnny asked, "Do I have to buy chips?"

"No sir, any legal currency will do. Gold, silver, or genuine U.S. paper greenbacks. Place your bets."

Two men had placed money on the king. Other imprints were covered by one man only. Two of the imprints weren't covered. "Pardon me," Johnny said, reaching between the two men and laying down two fifty-cent coins, "but I like kings."

Sure enough, the first card drawn was the king. The next, the winning card, was a jack, which was covered with only a twenty-five cent piece. Grinning to himself, Johnny left. He'd known the king would be the losing card. More money was bet on that card than on any other. It was too tempting. He'd played cards with some of the best, and he knew when a man was dealing holdouts. Yep, he thought, this dealer is no gambler. He's a thief, pure and simple.

The night was still young, so Johnny walked, looking at the faces of the women on the streets. He walked up Seventeenth Street and back down Sixteenth. At times he felt like apologizing to women who thought he was being flirtatious. But he didn't know what to say. He'd recognize Suzanne if he saw her, he was sure of that. She was one of the prettiest girls he'd ever seen, with her light

145

brown hair, bright blue eyes, small dimple on her chin, and wide smile, as pretty as Frances. She wasn't only good to look at, she could do anything—make a meal out of whatever was on hand, keep a clean house, milk a cow, handle a team. Alan Mitchell was a very lucky man. Johnny hoped he knew that and treated his sister accordingly.

Around ten-thirty he gave up. He wasn't even sure Suzanne was still in Denver. Her husband seemed to have the wanderlust. And if she was here, she'd be at home this time of night, taking care of . . . it suddenly occurred to Johnny that she could have children. He could be an uncle.

Oh, Lord, he wanted to see her. Was she looking for him? Had she gone back to the homestead? If she had, she would have found it abandoned. And she would have seen the graves. She would know then that Momma had died, too.

Oh, Lord.

Jake was right. The corner of Sixteenth and Blake was crowded with pedestrians at nine o'clock in the morning. Johnny stood in front of the Planter's House Hotel, in front of the wide porch, and waited. Jake came out of the crowd and stopped beside him.

"Pardon me, mister, got a match?" He still wore that brooding expression, and had an unlighted hand-rolled cigarette dangling from his mouth. He was dressed better this morning, still in working-man's clothes, but clean and neat. He'd even shaved.

"No sir, I don't," Johnny said politely. "I don't use tobacco."

"Pardon me sayin' so, sir, but you appear to be a stranger in town. Can I direct you somewheres?"

"Well, as a matter of fact . . ." Johnny let his voice trail off.

"Here's the plan." Jake talked lower. "This yahoo leaves that joint at three o'clock ever' night. He carries his plunder in a money belt that he tries to hide under his coat. Oh yeah, he carries a hogleg pistol, loaded and cocked. He carries it in his right hand with his finger on the trigger. Lord help the pug that tries to rob 'im on the street."

He paused to see if anyone else was listening. No one was. Johnny looked at the sky and allowed, "Surely it won't rain anymore for a while."

"Ever'thing's soaked." Jake's voice dropped again. "But I know whar he lives. He's got a clapboard house only four blocks from whar he does his thievin'."

"I get it," Johnny said. "We'll be waiting there when he gets home."

"Keereck. Got your robbin' clothes?"

"Yeah. When are we gonna do it?"

"Tonight. Meet you on the corner of Fourteenth and 'rapahoe. It's always dark on that corner, so keep your eyes peeled."

Speaking louder, Johnny said, "I surely do thank you for your directions, sir."

Then in a lower tone: "Tonight it is."

Chapter Seventeen

Johnny walked the streets again, studying the faces of all the women he passed. What else could a man do? How best to go about finding somebody? Alan Mitchell, he'd heard, was not a laboring man, more like a clerk of some kind, well dressed, well spoken. Almost every employer in the city hired paper shufflers. He couldn't ask all of them. But because he had nothing else to do, he stopped at two of the banks on Seventeenth Street and asked for Mr. Mitchell. He stopped in three of the stores on Sixteenth and asked the same question. No Mr. Mitchell. He stood on the street, watching people pass by. Finally, he had a dinner of corned beef and cabbage in a Sixteenth Street restaurant. Then he walked to the intersection of Fourteenth and Arapahoe and picked out a two-story house and an elm tree as landmarks so he could find his way there in the dark.

At the Great Northern Hotel, his room was still

stifling. He hadn't slept well the night before. For another fifty cents, the clerk assigned him a room on the other side of the hall. That room was a little cooler, but not much.

Lying on his back, hands under his head, he stared at the plaster ceiling and worried about the crime he was soon to commit. Another robbery. This time he'd be robbing a thief. Jake always had robberies on his mind. He was always planning something. He'd always planned carefully, but no matter how well a crime was planned, something could go wrong. Jake had nothing else to do. Johnny and Bertram Goodfellow had other occupations, but not Jake.

"Hmph." Johnny grinned at the ceiling, thinking about Jake. Of the three partners in crime, Jake was the only one who made no excuses. Johnny and Bert complained that they'd been stolen from by the law, and they were getting even. Jake admitted he was a criminal simply because he didn't want to work for a living.

"Hell," he'd once said, "I'm a good carpenter and a fair kind of blacksmith. I c'n get a job. I just don't want to. Robbin' is easier. And I c'n say for a fact I never took a dime from a workin' man."

Robbing was also a challenge, a risky adventure. Johnny had helped pull enough robberies by now that he was no longer nervous about it.

Nervous, no. Worried, yes. There was always that nagging at the back of his mind. This had to end one way or another. He'd be either shot in a robbery or shot by the Nashes.

A quarter moon put out barely enough light for him to find his way to Fourteenth and Arapahoe streets. The only lights came from the windows of the houses on the streets, and the shades were down on most of them. The only sounds were barking dogs off in the distance. While Johnny watched, the lights went out in the two-story house.

"Psst." It came from under the elm tree. Walking quietly, Johnny made his way over. "Is that you?"

"It's me," Jake said. "Did you bring your robbin' clothes?"

"I'm wearing them over my other clothes."

"Good. How about your shootin' iron?"

"I've got the Dragoon. What have you got?"

"A Smith-&-Wesson six-shooter, and I've got a couple pieces of rope I took off a freight wagon when nobody was lookin'."

"We're early, but that's better than being late."

"It's a couple blocks from here. Let's go. Be quiet."

They walked softly, Johnny following Jake's vague shape in the dark. There were no lights in any of the windows now. Jake turned down an alley, stopped, and whispered, "It's the second house from the corner, a three-room wood frame house. We'll have to break in the back. He always comes in the front door."

Johnny followed his partner until the dark shape of a house loomed before them. "There's a bedroom window right over here. If it's locked, I'll have to bust the glass."

"Won't the neighbors hear?"

"Don't think so. Here it is."

Groping with his fingers, Johnny couldn't help thinking how much easier crime would be if he had the night vision of an animal. It seemed they were always groping in the dark. He found the window, got his fingers under the bottom, tried pushing up. It was latched from inside.

"Shit."

"Tell you what," Johnny whispered, "I'll take this shirt off and use it to muffle the noise. I can put it back on." He unbuttoned the heavy cotton shirt, realized the white shirt he had on under it could be seen in the dark, and had second thoughts. "Damn it, I didn't think about that."

"All right, I'll use my shirt." A rustling of clothes, and Jake was holding his shirt against the window-pane. There was a tapping as Jake hit the glass with his pistol, then a louder tapping. The glass cracked. "Son-of-a-bitch."

"What happened.?"

"Cut myself. Hope I'm not bleedin'."

"Here, wrap my handkerchief around it." Johnny had to unbutton the waist of the oversized denim pants to get at a pocket of his wool pants. "Can you reach through?"

"Let's see. Nope. Gotta get some more of this glass outa here."

"Careful. Don't cut yourself again."

"I'm bein' careful." Then, "Yeah, here it is. Lift the window now."

The window opened. Jake crawled through on his stomach, and landed on his hands inside. "I'll unlatch the back door. I know where it is."

Johnny waited, glad that Jake had scouted the place, hoping that nobody had noticed him scouting the place. He saw the flare of a match inside the house, waited. "Psst."

In thirty seconds they were both inside, in total darkness. Jake whispered, "I watched through a winder a couple nights ago when he came home. First thing he did was light a lamp on a table near the front door. He had to put his gun down on the table to do it. That's when I'll jump 'im."

"Before or after he lights the lamp?"

With a mirthless chuckle, Jake said, "After. We cain't do nothin' in the dark."

"What do you want me to do?"

"I don't wanta have to outrassle 'im. Soon's I get aholt of 'im, stick that pistol up his nose."

"We have to find a place to hide close to the lamp table."

"When we hear 'im comin', I'll get behind the door. You stand against the wall beside the door. He won't see yuh till he lights the lamp, and I'll have holt of 'im by then."

"So we wait."

"Yup. Wait in the dark." They were silent. Johnny picked a spot against the wall next to the door. Another dry chuckle came from Jake. "Seems like we spend a lot of time waitin' in the dark."

"I was just thinking the same thing," Johnny said.

"Won't be long, 'less business is good at his tiger table. He won't leave as long as there're men to fleece."

"I hope this is a slow night at the faro game."

Waited.

Johnny whispered, "I can't see my watch, but I know it's after three."

"He would pick this night to stay late." Silence. Then, "I don't think I got all the glass outa my shirt. I'm gonna have to take it off and shake the hell out of it." Clothes rustled.

"Can't wear a shirt with glass in it," Johnny allowed. He heard Jake shaking the shirt.

"All right, I got 'er back on now. Feels better."

"Suppose he won't tell us where he's got his money hidden?"

"I dunno. I never beat on a man before. It has to be in this house somewheres."

"He ought to have enough on him to make this worthwhile."

"He will. But if we can, I'd like to find his stash."

"What will you do if he won't tell?"

"I dunno. What would you do?"

"I don't know either. I can't see torturing a man."

"Me neither. Scare hell out of 'im, but that's as fur as I ever went."

They waited.

"Shit, maybe he ain't comin' tonight. Maybe he's got a dolly somewheres he's spendin' the night with."

"There's always a chance that something unexpected will happen."

"Shit. It's tonight or forget it. He'll see the busted winder and know somebody was here."

"And we can't do anything about it."

Wait.

"God damn it. It's gonna be daylight purty soon." Silence, then, "Oh-oh. Somebody's comin'."

Johnny heard voices, low, coming closer.

"Son-of-a-bitch," Jake whispered, "he's got somebody with 'im."

Light laughter drifted in from outside. It was a woman's laughter followed by a man's chuckle.

"God damn," Jake whispered again. "I wish we c'd get outa here."

"Good or bad, we'll have to go through with it."

"We'll just have to play the cards the way they fall, Johnny."

"Yeah." Johnny also wished they could just get out. But a key was turning in the front door lock. He pulled a bandana up over his nose. It was too late now.

Chapter Eighteen

The woman spoke first. "Jeezus, it's dark in here."

"The lamp's right here," the man said. "Hold onto your foreskin."

Chuckles. "I ain't got no foreskin."

Something heavy was laid on the lamp table. Johnny hoped it was the man's gun. A match flared. Johnny recognized the dealer-banker's face. The woman was standing in the open door. Johnny thought, now is when it happens.

Jake waited until the lampshade was put back in place, then moved fast. Johnny timed his move with Jake's. Jake's arm went around the man's throat from behind and dragged him back, away from the gun on the table. In the same instant, Johnny gave the woman a hard shove away from the door and slammed the door.

The woman screamed. The dealer-banker swore. Johnny grabbed the woman from behind and wrapped an arm around her throat in the same kind of hold Jake had on the man. His arm cut off her scream.

Jake muttered, "This is a gun against yore head, mister. Shut up."

Johnny pushed the bore of the Dragoon against the woman's right temple, and said, "Shut up and stand still or I'll splatter your brains all over that wall." His bluff worked.

"Now," Jake said, his voice partly muffled by the bandana over his face, "git down on the floor, both of you."

Johnny released his hold on the woman and pushed her away. "Down. Get down or you're dead."

"D-don't shoot, mister." Her eyes were wide with fear. Her face was loaded with makeup, and she reeked of cheap perfume. "Please don't shoot."

"Get down, god damn it. On your bellies."

Muttering curses, the man got on his knees. Jake kicked him in the seat and barked, "On your belly." The woman didn't wait to be kicked. She immediately stretched out on the wooden floor, face down. She was slender, shapely. Now they both were stretched out.

Jake threatened, "One move and this cannon'll blow a hole in you." He pulled two short ropes from his belt and tossed one to Johnny. Johnny felt like apologizing to the woman, but he didn't. He had to keep her afraid for her life. He pulled her hands behind her back and tied them with a double square knot.

Straightening, he saw Jake pull the man's coat tail up, then his shirttail. A leather money belt was strapped around the man's waist. Jake unbuckled it and pulled it free. It was heavy with coins and paper money.

"All right. Now." Jake rolled the man over, sat astraddle him, and put the bore of his gun against the man's nose. "Where's the rest?"

"What rest?" His eyes crossed as they looked at the gun.

"Don't tell me you got a bank account," Jake sneered. "It's here in the house."

"It ain't. It's in the bank." His voice was strained.

"You're lyin' in your teeth. One more lie and you won't have any teeth."

Johnny took the pistol off the lamp table, squatted beside the woman's head, and showed it to her. "Ever see anybody shot in the head? The ball makes a bigger hole coming out than it does going in."

"Please. Don't hurt me. I ain't done nothin' to you."

Jake hissed through clenched teeth, "One more time, where is it?"

"I told you, I got a bank account."

"Say your prayers."

Speaking softly, Johnny said, "One shot will take off your nose. The next will take off your right ear, and the next will take off your left ear. You've been here before. Where does your friend keep his money?"

"Don't shoot me, please."

"Shut up, Mabel."

Jake forced the barrel of his gun into the man's mouth. "You shut up."

For a second, Johnny feared Jake was going to kill the man. He started to say something like, "Let's go now." But on second thought, Jake wouldn't shoot. The noise might bring the neighbors.

"All right, lady. Where is it?"

"I don't know. I never seen it. Honest."

Either they were good liars or they were telling the truth. The woman was so scared she was trembling, pleading, crying, "Please. Don't shoot me. Please." Tears ran off her cheeks onto the floor. A pool of urine spread from under her.

Johnny stood, feeling ashamed. He said, "She don't know where it is."

Jake stood too, muttered, "I oughta kill 'im. He cheated me outa two week's pay."

"You've got it back."

Removing the man's belt, Jake wrapped it around his ankles and buckled it. "Find somethin' to tie her legs."

Johnny used his own belt.

"Now," Jake said, "you're a lucky pair. We could've kilt yuh. Don't move, don't make a sound, or we'll kill yuh yet."

Looking down at the woman, Johnny said, "I apologize, lady. I really wouldn't have hurt you."

Jake blew out the lamp, opened the door. They left, walking quietly but rapidly in the dark.

They were silent until they reached the elm tree. Then, as they both stripped off their outer clothes, Jake said softly, "I muffed it."

"The unforeseen happened," Johnny said, unbuttoning the shirt.

"I didn't know he was bringin' a woman home with 'im, and I would've bet anything he had more money in the house."

"He might have, but I don't think he would have told us where."

"Not unless we beat 'im to a bloody mess."

"Well, we got something out of it without hurting anybody. They can scoot back-to-back and untie each other."

"Yeah. It'll take 'em a while. Meantime I got a cut on my hand, my right hand, and that's worrisome."

"Is it bad?"

"Not too bad, but what worries me is he'll see the blood on the busted winder and he'll know whoever busted it's got a cut hand."

"Uh-huh. And a cut on the hand is hard to hide."

"I reckon I'll ride out, Johnny—soon's it's light enough to find my horse at the livery barn over by the stockyards. I'll head north. I c'n buy some grub somewheres, and try to keep this hand out of sight. You can take the loot, if you want."

"No, you take it. I've got plenty of money."

"I'll see yuh in Cheyenne. We c'n divvy up there."

"Let me ask you, Jake, just out of curiosity—how come you said he cheated you out of two weeks' pay? Did you gamble with him?"

"Naw. Oh, I did a little piking, but I didn't lose much. I only said that so he'll spend the next two weeks tryin' to recomember who-all he's cheated."

Johnny chuckled. "He'll go crazy trying to figure out which one of his victims you are."

"So long, Johnny."

"See you in Cheyenne."

As Jake disappeared in the dark, Johnny bundled up the clothes he'd worn as a disguise. The Dragoon was in the middle of the bundle. He wasn't happy about the night's events. They'd got some money, but not much, maybe a few hundred dollars. What bothered him was the way he'd treated the woman. Shoving women around and scaring the pee out of them wasn't what he wanted to do. Feeling disgusted with himself, he walked to Larimer Street and the Great Northern Hotel.

He didn't leave Denver for two days. Something—only a vague hunch—but something told him Suzanne was there among the hordes of people in the territory's biggest and fastest-growing city. Because he could think of nothing else to do, he walked into the log police building off Fourteenth Street and asked help from a man in a blue uniform sitting behind a desk. No, the officer said, he knew of no one named Alan Mitchell, but he'd pin a note to a bulletin board, and maybe one of the officers knew him or knew of him. Come back tomorrow.

At the door, Johnny paused, thought it over, then went back to the desk. "I wonder," he said, trying to find a way to ask what he wanted to ask without inviting hard questions, "if the four men who robbed the Union Bank in Cheyenne a while back have done any bank robbing in Denver?"

"We got a telegraph about that Cheyenne robbery. Yeah, they fit the description of a gang that's robbed banks around here."

"Somebody said they could be the Nash gang."

"If it's the same bunch, and it prob'ly is, it's the Nash gang."

"How many men do you think are members of the gang?"

"Four or five. Why? What do you know about the Nash brothers?"

"Nothing. I just wondered."

The officer's expression showed he didn't entirely believe Johnny, but he didn't know what to do about it.

Johnny spent the rest of the morning watching people go by. Once, he saw a young, slender woman wearing a bonnet with a lacy edge come out of a drugstore and walk in the opposite direction. The bonnet hid her face. With long, fast steps, he got ahead of her, turned, and looked her full in the face. Disappointed, he said, "Pardon me, ma'am, I thought you might be someone else."

"Quite all right, sir." She smiled, and as she walked away she glanced back and smiled again. If I was the gentleman she thinks I am, Johnny thought, I might try to make something of this. But I'm not.

Shortly after noon, the *Rocky Mountain News* hit the streets. Johnny paid two cents to a boy in knickers and scanned the front page. Nothing interesting there. He found the story under a one-column headline on page three. Robberies were so common in the city that this one wasn't very interesting. But it did say one of the hoodlums apparently had cut his hand on the broken window glass, and police were searching for a man with a cut on his hand.

Jake was smart in riding out.

No new bank robberies were mentioned in the newspaper.

In a bar on Curtis Street, he paid a nickel for a glass of cool beer. The customers in here appeared to be mostly clerical workers, so he asked the bartender if he happened to know Alan Mitchell. No. He'd once known a gentleman named Albert Mitchell, but he was a middle-aged man. Johnny tried another bar where the customers wore stiff white collars and ties. Still no Alan Mitchell.

Outside, he felt a cool breeze blow off the high peaks to the west. The smell of rain was in the air. It reminded him of home, and how happy the Vorhes family was to have rain in August. Rain made everything grow, turned everything green. He and Suzanne used to dance in the rain, just for the fun of it. They behaved the way he and Frankie had in a creek north of Cheyenne. The rain had plastered Suzanne's hair to her head and soaked her dress. She laughed and did pirouettes in her bare feet. Johnny took running jumps and landed with both feet in the puddles, and laughed when muddy water splashed as high as his face.

Momma scolded them—but gently—for getting their clothes dirty.

Standing on the boardwalk, Johnny smiled at the memories. Then the smile faded, and he murmured to himself, "Where are you, Suzie?"

The rain started about sundown and continued off and on until sometime after midnight. He enjoyed the cool breeze that came through his hotel room window. In the morning, the streets were muddy again, but a bright sun promised to dry things out. The scent of tall pines drifted down from the mountains. Breakfast was bland. The cook had put too much flour in the pancake batter, and the bacon had been sliced too thin. Johnny went back to the police building, but got no encouragement. He spent another day watching people, then after supper he tried the drinking establishments again. In another bar which attracted the white-shirt crowd, he asked the same question, got the same answer.

Discouraged, feeling hollow, he stood at the bar and sipped his beer, deep in his own thoughts— until he realized that the man standing next to him was talking to him.

"Huh?" Johnny said. The man was stocky, with a bowler hat, a thin moustache, and a dark coat with wide lapels. "I said, wanna see some pictures?"

161

"Pictures? Of what?"

Leaning closer, the man put his hand inside a coat pocket and withdrew a sheaf of tintypes. "Nekked wimmen." He held the sheaf close where only he and Johnny could see them.

The women were naked, all right. Johnny blinked and swallowed at the shock of seeing pictures of women posing with absolutely nothing on. All he could say was, "Uh."

"Ever see anything like this? I can fix you up with any of 'em."

"Uh, how—where?"

"Over at Lucky Lou's. Down on the end of Curtis Street. She keeps only the purtiest, and she don't let no riffraff in."

"Oh."

"Lookit, there's a blond, a black-haired one, and a redhead. There's all kinds. Pick one."

Johnny looked as the man showed him one picture at a time. And suddenly his heart stopped. "Oh-o-o." His knees went rubbery.

"Whatsa matter, mister? You sick?"

All Johnny could do was groan and gasp for breath.

"Well, if you're sick, I'm leavin'."

"Wait," Johnny gasped. "Wait a minute." Feeling numb, lips trembling, he pointed a shaking finger. "That one. Who is she?"

"This 'un? I don't recall her name, but she's one of Lou's girls. Wanta meet her?"

He reached for the picture, then drew his hand back. He didn't want to touch it, but he couldn't pull his eyes away from it. The girl was beautiful, with full, shapely breasts, small waist, dark triangle, tapered thighs, a dimple on her chin.

Johnny was sick. Slowly, he turned and staggered from the bar. Outside on the plank walk, he almost threw up, fought to hold it down. He leaned against the building, groaning, wishing he could die.

"Suzie, Suzie, Suzie . . ."

Chapter Nineteen

It was a heartsick young man who boarded the northbound Denver Pacific. He hadn't slept at all. His mind was still reeling. He refused to believe it. It wasn't true; couldn't be. He should have gone to Lucky Lou's to assure himself that it was someone else. But he was afraid to. Scared. Scared of what? That it really was Suzanne?

Naw. Forget it. There were lots of young woman with dimples on their chins. And the black-and-white picture didn't show the color of her eyes. Suzanne had bright blue eyes. This girl's eyes could have been any color. Forget it.

Naw. No use denying it. It was Suzanne.

Johnny Vorhes rode silently, not hearing the man sitting next to him in the Pullman coach, trying to make conversation. Staring blankly out the window, he didn't see the country roll by, the low hills, the lines of trees. When someone came through the coach selling sandwiches and tea, he didn't even look up. His stomach was empty, but he felt no hunger. He felt nothing.

Not until the train stopped at Evans did he even realize where he was. Most of the passengers got off to stretch the cramps out of their bodies. Johnny got off, too, and went inside the derailed passenger car that had been converted to a café. He sat at the long counter and ordered roast pork and mashed potatoes, but he only picked at it.

Meal paid for, he went outside and walked east, away from the railroad yards, past the new house, past the barn. He heard the conductor holler, " 'Bo-oard," but paid it no mind. On the east side of the barn was a series of corrals. There were horses in the corrals. A long sign over the end of the barn read: "Hutchison's Stage & Freight."

Walking faster now, his mind working again, Johnny approached a lean, stringy man in bib overalls who was harnessing a team of big horses. "Are you Hutchison?"

"That's my name."

"Are you in the freight business?"

"Yup." Hutchison paused long enough to look at Johnny over the back of one of the horses. The horse would weigh sixteen hundred pounds, and the man had to stand on his toes to see over it. "Railroad don't go ever'whar."

"Got a saddle horse for rent?"

"I ain't in the livery business."

"Well, I need a horse, and I'll pay you for the use of one."

"How'd I know you'd come back?"

"Have you got a horse for sale?"

"Shore, I'll sell you a horse and saddle."

"Tell you what, you name the price and I'll put up the money. Cash. Then, when I bring the horse back, you give me my money back and I'll pay a fair price for using him."

"Hmm." Hutchison buckled the hames around the collar on a brown horse. That done, his eyes went over Johnny from the calfskin boots to the white shirt and homburg hat. "You from back East?"

"No. I've handled horses all my life."

"Well, seems fair enough. Put up a hundred bucks cash and I'll give you a good horse and saddle."

"That's a lot of money."

"What's the difference, if you're gettin' it back?"

"None, I guess. But let's go over to the café. I'd like to have a witness to our deal."

Thirty minutes later, Johnny was riding east on a stout sorrel mare, carrying a thick beef sandwich in a flour sack tied behind the cantle. Before he left, he strapped on the Dragoon and put his satchels in Hutchinson's office for safekeeping. He rode at a slow trot, and for the moment forgot the picture and everything else. It was mid-afternoon, and a late August sun warmed his shoulders and back, the horse had an easy gait, and it was good to be away from the cities, out where the only sound was the beat of the horse's hooves. The only thing manmade in sight was the wagon road he was following. As he neared a stand of trees, he heard the meadowlarks warbling their familiar tunes. He smiled, and realized he had missed those birds.

It was dusk when he saw Rollinsville ahead, and dark when he rode down the main street. He could see by lamplight in the windows that the town had grown a little. Now there were two cafés and a one-story clapboard building with a sign that read: "Rooms for Rent." Still no sidewalks, though. A few people on the street watched him ride by, but showed no recognition. At the stage and freight corrals, he knew the hostler, a man named Jules. But the hostler, except for a short appraisal, didn't give him a second thought.

His horse cared for, he walked, guided by lighted windows, to the "Rooms for Rent" sign. No, he wouldn't be recognized here. It had been three years. Or was it three-and-a-half years? In that time he'd filled out and was no longer a skinny kid. And he was well dressed, no longer the son of a poor dry-dirt farmer. He knew he looked strange in his city clothes, carrying the big Colt Dragoon, but stranger folks had passed through here.

The room he rented held only a narrow bed. There were a few nails on the walls to hang clothes from. He found the washbasin and bucket of water on a bench out back, and washed his face and hands. Supper in one of the cafés was fried chicken. These farmers almost lived on fried chicken. It was good. He'd decided to save his sandwich until tomorrow.

Shortly after daylight he was riding again, now angling to the south, heading for the Nash homestead.

It was what had happened to Suzanne that had brought him here. Suzanne was a . . . he couldn't bring himself to even think the word. And Frankie was gone. Death wasn't so fearful now. Living in fear was worse. Now was the time.

The Nash farm wasn't far, about six miles. Johnny was calm, ready. He rode out of a wide, shallow draw not far from the big barn and the two-room house. No cattle were in sight. A small patch of something was growing behind the house. Spuds, probably. Only one horse stood in a corral, but there could be more in the barn. Reining up, Johnny checked the loads on the Dragoon. He wished he had Jake's shotgun. He wished he had Jake. Jake would help. Too late. But with two of the gang in jail, maybe only the two brothers would be here.

Now was the time.

Riding at a walk, wide around the barn, he approached the house. Still nothing human in sight. They could be watching from a window. Thirty feet from the house he dismounted, keeping the horse between him and the house. He yelled, "Hello. Hello in there." The front door opened. Johnny's hand rested on the butt of the Dragoon.

The man who stood in the door wasn't one of the Nash brothers. He was no one Johnny had ever seen before. He squinted in the morning sunlight at Johnny.

"I'm looking for Powell Nash," Johnny yelled. "Or Court Nash."

"They ain't here." The man was old, round-shouldered, nearly bald.

"Do you know where I can find them?"

"Who are you?"

"My name is Vorhes. I used to be a neighbor."

"They ain't here much. I'm just holdin' down the homestead."

"Do you know when they'll be back?"

"I never know when they're comin' back."

"Are you here alone?"

"Yep."

Johnny didn't know how tense he was until he realized that nothing was going to happen. He felt weak as the tension drained out of him. "Will you tell them something for me?"

"Yep."

"Remember my name, Vorhes. Tell them I'll be in Cheyenne."

"I'll tell 'em."

Mounted again, Johnny rode north, trying to sort out his feelings. Relief was mixed with disappointment. In a shootout with the two Nash boys, he probably would have been killed. But unless the laws caught up with them, the shootout had to happen. He wished it had happened.

At noon, he picked up Wild Horse Creek, and turned the mare east toward the Vorhes homestead. He followed the creek a mile east, and reined up, astonished.

The dam he expected to see here was gone. Most of it. Both ends of it were still here, but the middle was gone. Washed out. What was more astonishing was the creek. It was back on its original course.

For the moment, the Nash bunch was forgotten. "Well, what? How come?" The sorrel mare cocked one ear back at him. "This do beat all."

He rode upstream a ways, noticed water-smoothed deadwood lying in the grass along the creek, and figured it out.

Talking to himself, he said, "Mother Nature didn't like the course Old Man Duran picked, so she knocked out that dam and sent the creek back where she belonged." Johnny laughed. "Boy, oh boy, the creek had to have been wide and wild to do that." Chuckling, he rode on downstream.

"Whatta you know about that? Ain't that something? Bet Old Man Duran had a shit hemorrhage."

Johnny was still chuckling when he rode over a rise and saw the Vorhes homestead.

Again he was astonished.

The sod loafing shed had been partially rebuilt with wood, and the corral was standing. The chickenwire fence was flat on one side, but the roosting house appeared to be solid. And from where Johnny sat his horse, the house looked the same as when he'd last seen it.

"Can't be," he muttered. Riding on, he discovered that the roof was sound, the window glasses were in one piece, and the door was closed and latched from the outside. Shaking his head, he muttered again, "Can't be."

He dismounted, tied the mare to one of the Dutch elms his mother had planted. Then, heart in his throat, afraid of what he might find, he unlatched the door and slowly opened it. Iron strap hinges squeaked. Johnny's jaw dropped open.

Except for a thick layer of dust, everything was the same. The four-burner cast-iron cook stove, the homemade table and chairs, the wooden shelves, the two bunks against a far wall . . . nothing had changed. Even the homemade quilts were on the bunks. Something had made a nest on one of the quilts, but no damage was done. And the wooden floor, when he walked across it, had a good, solid sound. In the other room, the two spring beds were made up, the long dresser sat solidly under a window, and the wire strung across one corner to hang clothes on was still there. Some of his mother's clothes were hanging from the wire.

For a long moment, Johnny was speechless. Finally, speaking almost reverently, he said, "Will wonders never cease?"

A closer inspection showed him a small water spot on the dusty floor. "One little leak," he said to himself. "We built that roof right." Tiny footprints were proof that mice had moved in, and were probably still there. Mice had gotten into the flour, sugar, and cornmeal sacks on the shelves.

But the roof could be patched, the mice could be trapped, and the groceries could be replaced. Johnny could only shake his head in disbelief.

When he went outside again, he got his first clue as to why everything was in good shape. The big meadow across the creek had been mowed. Half of it was cut; grass was stirrup-high on the rest. A mowing machine was sitting in the middle. Mounting the horse, he rode across the creek, discovered that old irrigation ditches had been cleaned out and the meadow irrigated. "Well, well."

At the corral, he got down and unsaddled the mare. It had rained since men and horses had been here, but some prints were visible in the dirt. There was even hay in a manger under one end of the shed.

"Had to have been Old Man Duran's crew," he said to himself. "But I can't see that they did any harm."

John Vorhes spent the night at the homestead where he'd grown up. He took a quilt off the bunk he'd slept on most of his life, carried it outside, and shook the dust off. His only meal was the sandwich he'd brought from Evans. The mare enjoyed a good feed of fresh-cut hay. Lying in bed, Johnny remembered when he and his dad had built the bedroom. He was thirteen then. Before that, the family of four had lived in one room. That was back when he and his sister rode a horse to school in Rollinsville. They had a big brown horse named Chigger that they worked in harness and rode bareback. When Poppa Vorhes needed Chigger to pull a plow or a cultivator, the kids walked to school. Chigger didn't mind carrying the two kids on his broad back, but Suzanne had complained about getting her dress dirty. Johnny was just as happy dirty as clean.

He recalled the blizzard that came up suddenly one day right after they'd started riding Chigger home from school. The temperature dropped to ten below zero, and the snow was blowing so thick they couldn't even see the horse's head. Hands and feet cold, faces numb, they soon lost all sense of direction, and didn't think they were ever going to get home. Johnny hung onto the horse's mane to keep from being blown off, and Suzanne hung onto Johnny. "We're lost," Suzie," Johnny had said. "We're gonna die out here." The wind almost took the words out of his mouth.

"No, we're not," Suzanne had said, riding behind him, her breath cold on his neck. "Just you hang onto this horse, Johnny. Hang on."

He'd hung on till he had no more feeling in his fingers. He had no feeling anywhere. He wanted to slide off the horse, curl up in the snow, and sleep.

"S-Suzie, I . . ." Snow was stuck to his face and lips. He couldn't talk.

His sister screamed at him, "Hang on, Johnny. Don't you dare fall off." She wrapped both arms around him. "The Lord will ·take care of us. Momma alway said the Lord would take care of us. Just you hang on, now."

It was Chigger that took care of them. They had no idea where they were until the big horse stopped at the corral gate. Poppa was there, waiting for them. He hadn't a chance in the world of finding them in the storm, but he couldn't stay in the house by the fire as long as his children were out in a blizzard.

Good old Chigger. He got old and swaybacked, and died of the colic. That's what Poppa Vorhes figured. Most old horses died of it.

Johnny slept until after sunup. He washed his

face in a bucket of water he'd carried from the creek. He was on his way to the corral to saddle the mare and lead her to water, when he saw men across the creek. Two were in a horse-drawn wagon and two were horseback. When they saw him, one of the men on horseback turned in his direction. Johnny wished he'd strapped on the Dragoon, and he considered hurrying back inside for it.

But the man called out, "Good morning," and was smiling as his horse splashed through the water. Johnny was suspicious and tense, but stood his ground.

Reining up, the man stayed on his horse, waiting for an invitation to dismount. "My name's Duran," he said, pleasantly. "James Duran. Mind telling me who you are?" Suddenly, his eyes widened as he looked closer at Johnny. "You're not ... you wouldn't be John Vorhes?"

"I am." Johnny recognized the name, but not the man. He remembered seeing young Duran only once, and he'd heard that the youngster, only a few years older than him, was going to school somewhere back East.

"I guess you don't remember me, John. I'm the son of Volney Duran. I remember seeing you in Rollinsville a few times."

"I remember Volney Duran." Johnny wasn't smiling.

"Yes. Well." Young Duran's smile vanished. "My father died a year ago last spring. I did some checking and found that you and your sister Suzanne own clear title to a hundred and sixty acres here, including that meadow."

Johnny hooked his thumbs in the waistband of his wool pants and waited for the other man to go on. "I, uh, when it became obvious that the place

173

was abandoned and no one was cutting grass off the meadow, I brought a mowing machine and some men over and harvested some hay. We can flood the meadow now and then and get two cuttings a year from it." Nodding in the direction of the mowing machine, he added, "This is the second cutting in three months."

Johnny still said nothing, waiting for the other man to speak again. Duran waited for Johnny to say something. Finally, Duran said, "If you're planning to move back in, we'll leave."

Beginning to realize now that young Duran was no threat, Johnny relaxed, and said, "What happened to the creek? Mr. Duran dammed it, you know, and turned the water away from here."

"I know." Young Duran sat straighter in his saddle. His horse, a gray gelding, shuffled its feet and pulled at the bit, wanting to move on. "You understand . . ." The horseman paused as if trying to think of the right words. "Mr. Vorhes, my father drove a herd of cattle to this territory long before the land was opened to homesteading, before there was a town or anything else for a hundred miles. He cut hay off that meadow with a scythe and watered his stock here. When your folks settled here, fenced off the meadow and creek, he felt cheated. He'd fought Indians—my mother was murdered by Indians—and he'd worked through summer droughts and winter blizzards to establish a cattle ranch. He believed this land belonged to him."

Another pause. Then Johnny said, "We worked hard, too. My dad worked so hard he ruined his health. But we had a pretty good little farm here until Mr. Duran built that dam. After that, we starved out."

Shaking his head sadly, Duran said, "I know. I

don't blame my father for what he did. I understand how he felt. But it was wrong. The dam will not be rebuilt."

Johnny absorbed that, then asked, "Sheriff Walson, is he still sheriff?"

"No. He failed to win reelection. I think he moved to Denver."

After absorbing that, too, Johnny said softly, "Care to get down?"

Ten hours later, John Vorhes was checking into his room at the Cheyenne Arms. The room was going to feel empty without Frankie. The desk clerk looked at him from under his eyeshade. "You're a friend of Mr. Goodfellow's, ain't you, the gentleman that owns Goodfellow's drygoods store?"

"Yeah."

"Too bad about him."

"What?" Johnny said. "What do you mean?"

"He was shot."

Chapter Twenty

Cheyenne had no hospital, but at their home Dr. Zimmerman and his wife kept a room available for the sick and injured who had no one else to care for them. Bertram Goodfellow was asleep when Johnny entered the room. He had a peaceful look on his face, but he was pale. He'd lost a lot of blood, the doctor had said, but he had a fifty-fifty chance of recovering. At first, the doctor was afraid the bullet had damaged the liver or ruptured the spleen, but during surgery he discovered that it had missed the vital organs.

The doctor, a thin, middle-aged man with a billy goat beard, said, "I don't think it advisable to disturb him now. He needs rest."

"Whatever he needs he can pay for," Johnny said, "and if he can't, I will."

"We're doing all we can. The next twenty-four hours are crucial, however. If you're a praying man, Mr. Vorhes, now is a good time for it."

Outside, under a cloudy Wyoming sky, he wished Momma Vorhes were here. She could pray. Johnny Vorhes? "Humph," he snorted. "Who would listen to a sinner like me?"

They told him about it at the Silver Bell. Two men had robbed Bert Goodfellow at his store and shot him. He was conscious long enough to tell Police Chief Tobias Wimmer about it. The descriptions he gave of the robbers didn't fit anyone in Cheyenne. Two names came immediately to Johnny's mind: Powell Nash and Court Nash.

Jonas Bark surmised, "Two hardcases passin' through saw his store open late, stuck a gun in his gut, and took what little money he had. They shot him and ran. How about some five-card draw, Vorhes?"

"When did this happen?"

"Last night. Doc Zimmerman operated on him most of the night. Got the lead out, but said he bled a lot. That's the way I heard it, anyways. We're gettin' a game up. Pull up a chair."

"Somebody saw two riders goin' south on a high lope," another man put in. "Hell, they're halfway to Denver by now. Set down, Vorhes, and let us take your money the honest way."

"Naw, not tonight."

He bought some newspapers and went to his room to read. He hadn't done as much reading lately as he should have, and he wished he had some of the books that Bert had sent for. Reading was a pleasure. Especially Greek mythology. The trick, Bert had said, was to read only the first syllables of the long, odd names. Otherwise you'd go crazy trying to pronounce them. Once he'd learned to do that, Johnny thought the stories were fascinating. Damnedest stories he'd ever heard—read.

Bert was propped up when Johnny went back about breakfast time. His hands were so weak and shaky he couldn't put a spoon to his mouth, so Mrs. Zimmerman was feeding him. When Johnny entered the room, Bert tried a weak smile.

"Don't talk," Johnny said. "Save your strength. I just wanted you to know I'm back. I'm fine. Jake's fine. I'll come again later."

Bert nodded and swallowed a spoonful of oatmeal.

"He's eating," Mrs. Zimmerman said. "The doctor said that's a good sign."

Johnny smiled at the patient. "He'll get well. I know him . . . he'll get well."

From there he went to Bert's house to make certain his and Bert's horses were cared for. A neighbor's two young sons had already fed them, but hadn't cleaned the corral. Johnny found a rake and raked the manure into a pile where it could be loaded into a wagon and hauled away. He got manure on his good calfskin boots, but grumbled, "A little clean horseshit never hurt anything." Then he rode his bay horse and led Bert's horse for six or eight miles out onto the prairie to give them some exercise. "You old ponies are getting too fat," he allowed.

Three-of-a-kind didn't beat a full house, and Johnny lost the biggest pot of the game. He should have guessed that the cigar-chomping railroad bigshot across the table had a full house. He couldn't seem to concentrate. Too many other things to think about: Bert, Suzie, Frankie. The Nash boys.

"Gentlemen, I'm afraid I'm gonna have to call it

a night." Pushing back his chair, he forced a grin. "At least you can't accuse me of not giving you a chance to win your money back."

"Thought you was a gambler, Vorhes."

"I'll be here tomorrow night, and you can give me a chance to win my money back."

Bert was improving. Now he could talk, but weakly. "Ironic, isn't it, Johnny? A robber shot by robbers."

Trying to make a joke of it, Johnny said, "It's getting so it ain't safe around here. Too damned many armed robbers."

"They were mad because I didn't have much money in the store. They didn't have to shoot me. What did they expect, anyway?"

"I heard your store was the only one open then, and the easiest mark. Everything else, the restaurants and saloons, were too busy, had too many men in them."

"Yeah. That's the way it was."

"Feel like telling me what they looked like?"

"Well, uh . . ." Bert's face blanched and he didn't finish what he'd started to say.

"Not now, Bert. Later. Rest."

It was seven-card draw again, and that railroad bigshot was smoking his cigar and blowing smoke in everyone's face. Johnny felt like shoving that cigar down his throat. His full house lost, but he was dealt four of a kind with the next hand and took the pot. It was a small pot, though. They'd guessed he held a winner. He was glad when the game broke up around two A.M.

On his way outside, he bumped shoulders with a man he saw out of the corner of his eye, and he turned to apologize. He turned just in time to see the blow coming and to jerk his head to one side.

Surprised, he blurted, "What the humped-up hell are you . . . ?"

The face opposite him was young, sneering, with a thin blond moustache. It was the face of a stranger. "You're that goddam gambler, ain't you? I hear you're tougher'n owl shit. Let's see how tough you are. Put up your dukes."

"Who the hell are you?" They stood close to the bar, and they were attracting a crowd.

"I'm the man that's gonna whip your ass, that's who I am." He wore a bowler hat and a better cut of clothes than the laborers. He also had a pistol in a Mexican holster on his right side, hanging low, butt tilted back. It looked like one of the self-cocking .38s. The stranger's fists were doubled and held in front of his face in a boxer's stance. A left fist shot out toward Johnny's face. Johnny stepped back out of reach and put his hands on his hips. Bowler Hat sneered, "Come on. Put up your dukes. Or would you rather shoot it out? Let's see how tough you are."

"Aw, for crying in the street. I don't feel like fighting."

"Hell you don't. You're a coward, that's what you are. Where I come from, men don't take them kinda insults. Put up your dukes."

Several thoughts went through Johnny's mind. He'd earned a tough reputation. He'd killed one man, fought a bullying detective to a draw with his fists, and taken a gun away from another. This young punk wanted to show everyone how tough he was by beating up a tough man. This kind of challenge was bound to happen. If he survived this, it would happen again. Johnny couldn't outfight everybody who came along. And he really didn't feel like fighting tonight.

But, as the punk had said, he couldn't just stand here and take insults. Knowing he was being forced into a fight started anger building in him.

"Listen," he said through clenched teeth, "you're packing iron. If you want to fight, why don't we do it right." He patted his belt. "You've got a gun, I've got a gun. If you want to fight, let's settle it once and for all."

"Oh ho, so you wanta shoot it out. Now you're talking my language."

Johnny knew then that he was being buffaloed into a life-and-death shootout, and he'd taken the bait. The punk didn't look it at first glance, but the way he carried his gun, and his sure-of-himself cockiness, marked him as a gunfighter. And he was here to kill Johnny.

At that realization, a cold fear rushed through Johnny. But it passed quickly, and he said, "Who sent you, one of the Nashes?"

A slight tightening of the jaw told him he'd guessed right. He could draw and shoot the .41 faster than most men could draw a gun from a hip holster, but not fast enough to outshoot a professional. He wished he were packing the Dragoon.

"You're the one that said something about guns, Vorhes. Go ahead, grab your iron."

Johnny hesitated. This wasn't the way he figured it would happen. He'd expected to go down in a fight with the Nashes.

"Piss on you," the punk sneered. "You killed a man with that gun, let's see you try it again." He stood spraddle-legged, right hand near the gun butt, ready.

The crowd was quiet, eyes going from one young man's face to the other's. Breathing shallow breaths, Johnny concentrated on drawing the belly gun.

Suddenly, it was over.

"Here, now—what's goin' on here?" Sheriff Rathke wasn't noticed until he stepped between the two young men. "If this's what it looks like, you'd both better cool down. Keep your hands away from them shootin' irons." The sheriff had his own gun out now. His face was hard. "The first one that shoots gets shot."

The punk relaxed, disappointed. Johnny relaxed, relieved.

"I know Vorhes here, but who are you?"

"I'm a stranger in town, but that don't mean I have to take insults from tinhorn gamblers."

"What's your name?"

"Langly. Jim Langly."

A made-up name, Johnny thought.

"Wal, Jim Langly, and you, too, Vorhes—if either one of you is found shot I'll know who done it, and you'll be arrested for murder. Get it?"

"I've committed no crime," Jim Langly said, "and I'm leaving." He stepped around the sheriff and went out the door.

Turning cold eyes on Johnny, Sheriff Rathke said, "You're just trouble lookin' for a place to happen. I wish you'd get out of my jurisdiction."

With a long sigh, Johnny said, "Right now I'm going to bed."

Bert was stronger. As soon as Mrs. Zimmerman left the room, he motioned Johnny closer. "Have you taken a look at our stash? I'm a little worried about it, what with the neighbors feeding our horses and all."

"Think they'll get nosy?"

"They probably won't, but you know me, I'm a worrier."

"I'll take a look."

"You can move into my house if you want to. You'd be doing me a favor if you did. Help yourself to anything in it."

"By the looks of you, I'd guess you'll be getting out of here pretty soon."

"In a couple days. I might need someone to stay with me awhile. Would you do that?"

"You bet. I'll move my stuff over to your house today, and tell the neighbors they won't need to feed the horses anymore."

"Good."

"Feel like describing the two hardcases?"

"Won't do any good. They're long gone."

"Do you remember what they looked like?"

"Exactly. I'll know them if I ever see them again, even if it's ten years from now. They didn't have to shoot me."

They were interrupted by the doctor's wife, who said, "He's improving, but he needs his rest."

"See you later, Bert."

He packed his two satchels and carried them to Bert's four-room house. Before he left the hotel, he made certain the clerk knew where to find him in case Frankie came back, or wrote a letter, or sent a telegram. Then he went to the closest neighbors and told them he was moving into Bert Goodfellow's house and not to get excited when they saw a lamp lighted at night. That done, he uncovered their stash.

Bert had it well hidden. Knowing that if anyone searched the place they'd tear the house apart, and that if he buried it outside, fresh dirt would make it easy to find, Bert had figured out a better spot.

He'd buried it in a tin box under the hay manger in his stable. As a businessman, he'd been able to take the gold coins to the bank a handful at a time and convert them to paper money, saying they were sales receipts. Paper money seemed to be accepted everywhere now, and was easier to handle. Johnny would have to do a little digging to reach the box, but as Bert had said, horses' hooves would soon tramp down any sign of digging. He'd also said there was no perfect spot, and twice a day he'd studied his hiding place to be certain that nothing had been disturbed.

Johnny used a long-handled slotted spoon from the kitchen to dig it out. It was all there. He put it back, replaced the dirt, forked some hay into the manger, and took the spoon back to the house. A shovel would have been a clue if anyone had come looking for a stash.

Not wanting to cook and wash dishes, Johnny took his supper at Reuben's, then went to the Silver Bell to find a game. Jonas Bark quipped, "I dunno, Johnny. You ain't safe to be around. Seems like some gunsel is always pickin' a fight with you."

"I draw trouble like spoiled meat draws flies, but I've got money here I ain't lost yet. Whatta you say?"

"Five-card draw or stud. None of that seven-card crap."

"Suits me."

Win a little, lose a little. Tonight Johnny won a little. When the game broke up around three A.M., after the chairs were pushed back and the table was vacated, Johnny shoved his money into his coat pockets, had one shot of whiskey at the bar, and went to Bert's house. He'd learned something from the faro dealer in Denver: when you walk around in the dark with money in your pockets, you'd better have a gun in your hand. Too, there was that punk Jim Langly. Though Johnny hadn't seen him but once, he suspected he was still in town. He carried the .41 in his right hand, cocked, finger on the trigger. No one bothered him.

In two more days Bert was able to leave the doctor's house. Johnny had the buggy waiting at the door for him, and had his bed made up and ready for him at home. Johnny even cooked supper, potato-and-sausage soup. He'd bought the bread and butter.

"Not what you'd call damned good, but plenty palatable," Bert allowed, sopping up the last of the soup with a piece of bread. "How did you learn to cook? I mean, you said your mother and sister were good cooks, so why did you learn?"

"My momma said she wasn't raising any helpless kids," Johnny replied, "and she kept me in the house sometimes and made me cook whether I wanted to or not."

"Lucky for me she did. The winter we stayed in that cabin over west, you had to do most of the cooking."

"I never liked to cook, but, yeah, I'm glad I learned something about it."

"Me, I can fry eggs and bacon, and that's about all."

After supper they talked, and Johnny told his friend about Suzanne. It made Bert unhappy. "I don't know what to say, Johnny. I wish I could say something, but I don't know what to say."

"No use talking about it."

"Maybe . . . Johnny, you said you haven't seen nor heard from your sister for years. You don't know . . . she could have gone through hell in that time. You can't know what-all might have happened to her."

Sitting with his elbows on the table, his chin in his hands, Johnny said, "Yeah," gloomily.

"No, I'm serious. Some old Indian once said something like, 'Don't judge your neighbor until you've walked a mile in his moccasins.' Or something like that. Maybe it wasn't an Indian. But it's pretty good advice."

"That picture . . ." The younger man could only shake his head.

"Could it be someone else? Some people don't look much like themselves in a photograph."

"I've thought about it and thought about it. It's Suzie."

"Well, there's that part in the Bible where someone said something like, 'Let him who is without sin cast the first stone.' Or something like that. Maybe it isn't in the Bible. I could have read it somewhere else. It makes a lot of sense, and it could apply to you, you know."

"Yeah, well." Johnny didn't want to talk about it anymore then. "Tell me about the sons-of-bitches who robbed you. What did they look like?"

They were easy to describe. The bigger of the two had a nose that had been broken and a tooth missing right in front. Dark hair. The other, the one who shot him, had a short, pug nose, thick lips, and a small scar through his left eyebrow. There was no use describing their clothes. They'd change clothes.

No further description was needed anyway. Johnny knew who they were.

He considered telling his friend about the Nash boys, but didn't. Instead, he said, "You'd better get in there on that bed. I'll fetch one of your books and light the lamp in there. You can blow out the lamp when you want to."

But Bert's words weren't wasted. After hours of lying in bed that night, worrying, Johnny broke the news at breakfast. "As soon as you're able to take care of yourself, I'm going back to Denver."

Looking at him over the rim of his coffee cup, Bert said, "You are?"

"Yeah. I'm gonna find Suzie. I have to see her."

Chapter Twenty-one

John Vorhes couldn't leave Cheyenne as long as his friend needed him. He cooked, washed dishes, swept the floors, and helped Bert to the toilet out back. At night he played poker in the Silver Bell Gaming House. He won more than he lost, and each night as he walked in the dark to Bert's house he had money in his pockets—and a gun in his hands.

It was when the card players took a break so Johnny could go outside and drain his bladder that he next saw Jim Langly.

He was on his way back, buttoning his pants, when a man stepped out of the shadows. There was that ratcheting sound of a gun being cocked. Johnny froze.

"Gotcha now, John Vorhes."

"Who . . . ?" Then Johnny recognized the bowler hat. "Mister," he said, "I've got a low opinion of the

Nashes, but I thought they'd do their own shooting."

"Maybe they don't want to be seen around here."

"So they hired you."

"Correct. Unless you want to raise the ante."

"My money is all inside on a table."

"That's your tough luck."

"You'll be hung for murder."

"Ha." The .38 was pointed at Johnny's face.

Then another voice came out of the dark, and another gun was cocked. "This's a big powerful shootin' iron behind yuh, mister. If yuh don't drop that peashooter in two seconds, you're gonna be dead."

The .38 hit the ground.

"Now, I'm gonna tell yuh somethin', mister. If I ever see yuh again I'm gonna kill yuh on sight. Hear? If you got a brain cell in your head, you'll get your sorry ass on one a them locomotives and make yourself hard to find. Hear?"

"Y-yessir."

"Git. Run."

He ran, quickly disappearing in the dark.

Johnny heaved a sigh of relief and said, "How've you been, Jake?"

"Tolerable. How's Bert?"

"He's getting better every day. Pretty soon he'll be as good as new. Did you have any trouble getting out of Denver?"

"Naw. I got out ahead of the newspapers. Took my time. Find your sister?"

"Uh." Johnny didn't want to talk about it, not here, not now. He changed the subject. "You just saved my life. How did you know?"

"I was drinkin' at the bar. I spotted you, but I

hoped you wouldn't spot me and say anything. There was some talk about you and that young rooster havin' a serious disagreement t'other night, and when I seen 'im foller you out, I follered him. I come out the front door and snuck around back here."

"I'll be damned. Does anybody know anything about him?"

"Reckon not. He just showed up."

"Bert will be happy to see you. He's holding some money for you."

"I'll drop in on 'im, but not tonight. He's prob'ly gone to bed anyways."

Bert was making his own way to the toilet now, and was reading a newspaper, sitting at the kitchen table, while Johnny peeled potatoes and sliced carrots for their supper. A knock on the kitchen door had Johnny suddenly looking for a gun. The knock came again.

"I don't think it's anything to worry about, Johnny. Probably a neighbor."

He was right. When Johnny opened the door he found a plump gray-haired woman wearing a plain blue apron standing there. She was holding a cast iron pot in both hands. The pot was hot enough that she had wrapped towels around the handles.

"I'm Mrs. Givens from down the street," she said. "I apologize for not bringing something sooner."

Bert put his newspaper down and hobbled to the door. "Mrs. Givens, how nice. Won't you come in?"

Stepping timidly inside, she said. "This is a casserole of beans and ham. I should have brought something as soon as I heard you was back home, but with five kids and a husband to cook for, I . . . I apologize."

Johnny took the pot from her hands and put it

on the stove. Bert dropped into his chair and said, "Why, that's certainly nice of you, Mrs. Givens. I'll pay you for it, and I'll pay your kids for taking care of our horses."

"Oh, no. We don't want no pay."

"Won't you sit down, Mrs. Givens? Johnny's coffee isn't too bad."

When she took another look at Johnny, her pleasant expression changed to a quick frown. She'd heard of him. "Thank you just the same, but I've got to get back."

Bert's eyes followed her to the door. "Thanks very much. It's wonderful to have such good folks for neighbors."

"You're welcome, Mr. Goodfellow. If we can be of any help, just holler."

"Well, isn't that nice?" Bert said after Johnny had shut the door. Shaking his head in wonderment, he continued, "I'd almost forgotten, Johnny, how many good people there are."

"There are some. I met a man just a few days ago that I thought was my enemy. Now I think he wants to be a good neighbor."

"My neighbors, people around here, look upon me as a respectable businessman." After a short pause, he added, "You know, I like that."

"I could tell she ain't got a very high opinion of me."

"Your occupation is more visible. My other life is known only by me, you, and Jake."

"My momma told me once the way to keep peeled spuds from turning dark is to put them in cold water. These will keep. That kettle she brought sure smells good."

Before they could start eating supper, there was another knock on the door, a soft one. A girl child stood there, holding a covered pan. "My momma told me to bring this over for Mr. Goodfellow. It's hot cornbread."

Bert came to the door. "Why, thank you kindly, miss. My name is Bert, what's your name?"

"Bessie Canfield." She smiled a timid smile, displaying a gap in her upper teeth.

"Where do you live, Bessie?"

"Yonder." She pointed to the next house west.

"Well, I thank you for bringing this over, and tell your mother I thank her. Will you do that?"

"Yessir." She turned and skipped happily away.

Supper was delicious, the best meal either man had had in a long time. But Bert was quiet, deep in thought. Not until their meal was over and Johnny had put some water on the stove did Bert speak.

"I hope Jake has no more plans that include me."

"Why?" Johnny asked, looking his way.

"I've been doing some serious thinking. Johnny, I don't want to be a criminal any more."

"Oh." Knowing that Bert wanted to talk, Johnny sat at the table again.

"I've got a good business, I've got money in the bank, and I've got a stash. Can you understand, Johnny? I want to be what folks think I am. I no longer want a secret life. Can you understand?"

"Yeah," Johnny said, thoughtfully. "Yeah, I know what you mean."

There was still no word from Frankie, no letter, no telegram. That was the last thing Johnny checked on before he said goodbye to Bert.

"Come and visit, Johnny. There's no one I'd rather visit with. If you ever need anything, anything at all, just let me know. Send a telegraph, send a letter, come yourself, just let me know."

They shook hands. "I'll do it, Bert."

He rode his bay horse south, carrying a blanket, a length of bed tarp, and one carpetbag on his saddle. An accumulation of robbery loot was stuffed into a money belt around his waist. He'd left his homburg hat and fingerlength coat behind, and was wearing new duck pants and a battered wide-brim hat he'd bought two years before. At Evans, just before dark, he arranged with Hutchison to leave his horse and saddle there for a few days. After a night in Hutchison's barn, he ate breakfast in the old passenger coach converted to a café. Hutchison joined him at the counter.

"Might rain," the older man said. "Might not. Cain't predict the weather in these parts."

"I was wondering," Johnny said around a mouthful of biscuit, "you said you've got horses for sale, have you got a light team and a wagon?"

"Sure have. Freight business is fallin' off, now that the railroad is goin' all the way to Denver, and I've got horses and wagons of all kinds to sell. You in the market?"

His words reminded Johnny of the stage robberies he'd helped pull. He wondered if he'd robbed Hutchison. Not likely. Money on the stages didn't belong to the stage owners. He answered, "Not just now, but I might be in a few days."

"Come around. I'm askin' fair prices."

They heard the southbound's steam whistle before they saw it coming. All they saw at first were puffs of black smoke, like Indian smoke signals. Then the big engine with its funnel-shaped smokestack and plow-shaped cow catcher chug-chugged into sight, whistle screaming to let everyone know she was coming. Number 48, pulling two passenger coaches and a string of freight cars, screeched and hissed its way to a stop at the water tank mounted on high wooden legs. She no more than stopped when the fireman was on top of the tank, wrestling a big spout into place over the locomotive boiler. When he pulled a chain opening a valve, water pressure caused the spout to jerk and buck, and the fireman had to hang onto it with all his strength to keep from being knocked off the tank. The passengers got out of the coaches to stretch. Johnny got on board.

The train started moving with three short toots of the whistle and a series of jerks that snapped the passengers' heads back. Sitting on the mountain side of the coach, Johnny idly watched the scenery roll by. He grinned inwardly when he saw the twin peaks on the skyline away over west and remembered what Jake had called them: "Squaw tits."

It was before one of their stage robberies. They'd picked out a spot due east of them. "We'll stop 'er right east of them squaw tits," Jake had said.

This wasn't a pleasure trip for Johnny. She might not want to see him. She'd be so ashamed at having him find her there that she might faint. Or run away. He tried to think of the best way to approach her and what to say. Nothing came to mind. As the iron wheels clickety-clacked over the fishplates that held the ends of the rails together, a deep sorrow filled his chest. He didn't know what he was going to do or say when he got there.

He wasn't sure he should go there.

Chapter Twenty-Two

So many guests checked in and out of the Great Northern Hotel that the clerk didn't remember John Vorhes. That was all right with Johnny. The room he was assigned was on the side opposite the brick building next door, and Johnny went right back downstairs and objected.

"Nobody can sleep on that side of the building in the summer," he said.

The clerk threw up his hands in resignation. "Some folks say it's too hot on the south side, and some say it's too noisy on the north side. Which do you prefer?"

"Noise is something I'm used to."

Another helpless shrug. "I'm sorry to say there is nothing available on the north side. Believe me, this job is easier in the winter."

"Yeah," Johnny groused, "it probably is."

He couldn't have slept much anyway. Worrying about what he might find the next day kept him awake. He lay on top of the bed in his shorts and worried. And sweated. By early morning the room had cooled some, and he slept. But when he awakened at sunup he was as tired as when he'd gone to bed.

Breakfast could have been delicious, but it would have made no difference. Everything tasted like paper. He sat hunched over his meal at a café counter, barely aware of where he was. A rough voice jerked him awake.

"I said, pass the sugar."

"Huh? Oh, pardon me." He reached for the sugar bowl on his right and slid it down the counter.

"Whatsa matter, been whorin' all night?"

The word struck the wrong nerve. The nerve stretched as tight as a banjo string, then snapped. "What? What did you say?"

The man was big, in a bill cap and overalls. "God damn it, do I have to say ever'thing twice? I said, been whorin'?"

Without thinking, Johnny backhanded him smack across the mouth. He swiveled on his stool and followed the left hand blow with a right cross to the jaw. The big man fell backward off his stool.

"Get up," Johnny hissed, standing over him. "Get up so I can knock you down again."

Another man, wearing a dirty white apron and a white cap, came running around the counter. "What's the matter with you? You crazy? I heard what he said. He didn't say nothin' insultin' a-tall. You're crazy, mister."

Johnny dug a handful of coins out of his pocket, slammed them down on the counter, spun on his heels, and stomped out.

He was halfway down the block before he realized what he'd done. When it came to him, he stopped, looked back. Silently, he asked himself, What in hell did you do that for, John Vorhes? You ought to go back and apologize. He turned in that direction, then stopped. No; if he went back, his apology wouldn't be accepted, and he'd be in a fight. A fight was the last thing he needed. He hoped the man wasn't hurt. Probably wasn't. Just got caught off balance, is all.

Walking back to the Great Northern, he shook his head sadly and muttered to himself, "That was a crazy thing to do. John Vorhes, you are crazy."

In his room, he lay on his back, hands under his head, and stared at the ceiling. What to do? How to do it? When? The ladies at Lucky Lou's no doubt slept late. How late?

Lordy, lordy.

He felt like getting on a train and going wherever it went. They went in almost all directions these days. North, south, east. Just get the hell away from this territory. Forget everything and everybody. He could buy a ticket to California if he wanted to. He had his share of the loot in a money belt, and he could live a long time without earning a dime. Do anything he wanted to do.

Run. Leave all this behind.

He shook his head and mumbled to himself, "No. She might need help. She might need me.

"She might not."

Finally, he got up, splashed cold water on his face, and combed his hair. By now, somebody ought to be up at Lucky Lou's. "All right, John Vorhes," he mumbled, "let's get this over with."

Lucky Lou's was easy to find. A man on the street pointed out the place. It was a two-story frame house, painted white, with a big bay window in front. Heavy velvet drapes had been pulled across the window. Johnny stepped uncertainly onto the porch, up to a big door with etched-glass panes. He twisted a winged button, which jangled a bell inside. He waited for someone to open the door. He twisted the button again. The bell inside sounded again. Still no sign of life. Again he rang the bell. Finally the door opened a crack and a black face appeared.

"Go 'way. Ever'body's in bed." It was a woman's voice.

"I'm looking for somebody," Johnny said. "I apologize for bothering you, but I'm looking for Suzanne Vorhes."

"Who you lookin' for?"

"Suzanne Vorhes. I mean Mitchell. Suzanne Mitchell."

"We ain't got no Suzanne Vorhes or Mitchell."

"She was here. Is she still here? She hasn't moved on, has she?"

"I tol' you, we ain't got nobody by that name."

Johnny lied, "I've seen her." Silently, his hopes rose. Could it be that Suzanne was never here? He wanted to believe that, but he had to be sure. "Maybe she's using another name. She's about five feet, four inches tall, twenty-three years old, brown hair, blue eyes. She's got a dimple in her chin."

The black face pondered that. "I'll go fetch Miz Lou. You wait out here." The door slammed.

It was a long wait, worse than waiting for the train at Hillsdale. It's a mistake, he told himself. It's a terrible mistake. Suzie ain't here. Never was. It has to be a mistake. The door opened.

"Who are you?" The woman standing in the door was almost as wide as she was tall, and was covered from chin to floor with a pink silky robe. Her blond hair was coiffed in fingerwaves around her face.

"Pardon me, ma'am. I'm sorry to bother you this early. My name is John Vorhes. I'm looking for my sister Suzanne Vorhes. Her married name is Mitchell." Please, he pleaded silently, tell me you never heard of her.

Instead, the woman said, "Come in."

The heavy drapes kept most of the light out, and the room was in semidarkness. Johnny was standing on a thick carpet, surrounded by heavily padded furniture. An oak bar was in a far corner with liquor bottles of all kinds arranged on a shelf behind it.

"You're Suzanne's brother, you say?"

"Yes, ma'am." Johnny's heart sank as he stood there, twisting his hat in his hands.

"We call her Kitty."

"Yes, ma'am." He swallowed a lump in his throat. "Can I see her?"

Speculative eyes searched his face. "All right. Come with me."

He followed her up the carpeted stairs to a hall. She stopped at the last door. "Wait here." She opened the door barely wide enough to slip through.

His heart pounded. Oh God, oh God.

The door opened wider, and the fat woman beckoned. "Come in. She's sick. She's very sick."

In spite of the semidarkness and the white sheet that covered her to her chin, he recognized his sister: the light brown hair, the dimple in her chin. Her eyes were closed, but opened slowly, then suddenly wider. The voice was weak. "Johnny? Is that you, Johnny?"

"Yeah, Suzie, it's me."

"Johnny, oh my God." The blue eyes squeezed shut. Tears ran off her face into a white pillow.

"Suzie, it's . . . ." He wished he could find the right

words. "It's all right. I'm here to help you." He felt like crying himself.

"O-o-h, Johnny." She cried.

Turning to the fat woman, Johnny asked, "What's wrong with her?"

"We don't know. The doctor don't know."

"Who's the doctor?"

"Doc Mowbry. He doctors all my girls. We're doing the best we can for her."

"Where is he?"

"Over on Arapahoe, next to Seventeenth."

He wanted to touch his sister, hold her hand, but her hands were under the sheet. "Susie, it doesn't matter what's happened. Don't worry about anything. Don't worry about anything at all. I'm here to help you. I'll be right back."

"Johnny, I'm so . . . ." She blinked back tears and sniffed. "I'm so . . . ."

He didn't let her finish. "It doesn't matter. All that matters is getting you well. I'm gonna go see the doctor, and I'll be right back."

Turning, he went to the door, stopped, looked back. "It doesn't matter, Suzie. Remember that."

He found the doctor's office in a one-story building on Arapahoe Street, but he had a long wait to see the doctor. The waiting room was full, and a middle-aged woman in white clothes and a white cap fixed a stern look on him and demanded:

"What seems to be your trouble?"

"Oh, uh, nothing. I'm here about my sister. Doctor Mowbry has been attending my sister, and I'd like to talk to him about her."

"Very well. The doctor will see you shortly."

Sitting in a straight-backed chair, he crossed his legs one way, he crossed his legs another way, he stretched his legs out in front, he pulled his feet under the chair. Most of the other patients were children, there with their mothers. One was crying softly. The others were quiet. An overweight young woman unbuttoned her dress and let one breast flop out so her baby could nurse. Johnny quickly looked away.

"John Vorhes? The doctor will see you now."

He followed the nurse into an examination room, but stood, waiting. Dr. Mowbry, when he came in, looked a lot like Dr. Zimmerman at Cheyenne; the same thinning hair and the same billy goat beard. "What can I do for you, young man?"

Johnny explained. The doctor listened, then nodded. "Suzanne Mitchell, you said? They don't often give their real names over there, but for the record, I . . . you're her brother?"

"Yessir. How sick is she?"

With a shrug of his shoulders, the doctor said, "She's ill. Her high fever indicates a virus of some kind, but I don't think that in itself is her main problem. I think she's just . . . I think she's just tired of living. Perhaps you can give her some hope."

Remembering how his mother had died, Johnny shook his head sadly. "Do you mean . . . ?" He didn't know how to phrase the question.

"It's not uncommon. Women in her . . . Mr. Vorhes, do you know about Lou's house, what it is?"

"Yessir, I know."

"It's not uncommon for women in Miss Mitchell's, uh, profession to lose interest in living. They see their older sisters, what they have become, too old to attract a man, begging for food, for a place to sleep, and they see themselves ending that way. Too many of them take their own lives."

"Can she travel? I'd like to take her home."

"She is weak. I don't think she can survive a long journey. A short one, perhaps." The doctor stroked his beard, looking at the floor. "It would be better, much better, if she left that place. As a matter of fact, she must leave that place. But she is weak. She will need good care and time to recuperate. How much time, I cannot say. It depends on . . ." Again the doctor shrugged.

"Suzanne is a strong woman," Johnny said. "I'm taking her home."

Chapter Twenty-three

From the doctor's office, Johnny went to the Denver Pacific depot and learned that the trains ran north one day and south the next. Otherwise they'd run into each other. The northbound had pulled out that morning. His next stop was Lucky Lou's.

"She ain't leaving till somebody pays me," the silk-gowned fat woman said.

"What do you mean, pays you?"

They stood in the parlour. The drapes were still closed, telling all outsiders that the house wasn't yet open for business. "What I said. She's been sick for two weeks and ain't earned a dime. She owes me, and nobody owes me for very long."

"How long has she been here?"

"Only a month. Been here a month, and sick ten days of it. I ain't running a poor farm here."

"How much do you figure she owes?"

Speculative eyes studied Johnny's face. "How much money have you got?"

"That's none of your business."

"All right, five hundred dollars."

The figure was a surprise, but Johnny absorbed it with no change of expression. "That's too much. That's robbery."

Lucky Lou snapped, "No, it ain't. I paid two hundred dollars for her, and she's been occupying a room that could have been occupied by a moneymaker." Silver bracelets on her wrist jingled as she waved toward the second floor. "Besides, I had to pay the doctor. I ought to make it six or seven hundred dollars."

"If I don't get her out of here, she'll die."

"So be it. She won't be the first to go from here to the graveyard."

"You're full of generosity for the girls who work for you, ain't you?"

"I'm not taking any shit from you, either, or anyone else. The price just went up."

It was robbery. No doubt in Johnny's mind about that. He could pay it if he had to. But he hated the slick unarmed kind of thieves like her. He hated them more than he hated the hoodlums. It was an unarmed thief who'd ruined the Vorhes family farm, ruined the Vorhes family. Anger was building in him fast.

Keep it down, John Vorhes, he told himself.

"Well, I'm going up to see her."

"You can see her, but she ain't leaving till I get my money. And if you think you can just carry her out of here without paying me, think again."

Lucky Lou turned her head and yelled, "Mac, Joe, come out here."

A door on the other side of the room opened and two men came through. Big men. Big-shouldered men. Men with square, hard faces, billy clubs in their hip pockets, and six-shooters on their hips.

Lucky Lou cocked her blond head to one side. "Need I say more?"

Johnny was unarmed. He got the message, but he wasn't giving up. "I don't know much about the law, but I'll bet it's against the law to keep somebody against her will."

"Well then, Mr. Smartass, why don't you go to the law?"

It didn't take Johnny long to get that message either. She was paying the police. Shrugging with resignation, he said, "I'm gonna talk to my sister. We'll figure out something."

"You do that. You figure something out. But remember this: we've carried men out of here before. Them that survived went to jail for disturbing the peace. Remember that."

"Yeah, sure," Johnny grumbled.

Upstairs, he opened the door to Suzanne's room carefully and peered around it. Her eyes were closed, but she opened them when she heard the door creak. She moaned, "Johnny, how did you know? Why did you come?" I'm so ashamed, I could die." Her eyes filled with tears.

In three long steps he was at her bedside. "Never mind any of that, Suzie. We're going home, you and me. At home you can get well."

She tried to sit up, fell back. "Home. I can never go home."

"Oh yes, you can. Suzie, I was there, at the farm, just a couple of weeks ago. Everything's the way I left it. We can just move right in."

"I can't. Why don't you leave and just let me die?"

"Yes, you can."

"No. I went there for a visit a year ago. I saw momma's grave. There's nothing there."

"There is. It's all there." He tried to put some enthusiasm in his voice. "You won't believe what happened, Suzie. The creek's back in front of the house. Wild Horse Creek. Mother Nature knocked that dam out and sent the water back where it belongs."

Suzanne's eyes widened a little, but not much.

"That's not all. Old Man Duran is dead. His son—remember James Duran?—he's running the ranch now, and he promised that the dam won't be rebuilt. And if we don't want to farm the place, Suzie, I've got enough money that we can live there in comfort a long time, and you can get well."

Again she tried to sit up. Again she fell back. "No, Johnny, it's too late for me. Just let me die."

"No. I won't do that. Remember, Suzie, when we were caught in a blizzard, and I wanted to just fall off Old Chigger and die? Remember how you wouldn't let me, how you held me on? Well, I'm not gonna let you die."

Shaking her head slowly, she said, "Johnny, Johnny."

"Tell me something, Suzie, not that it matters—but how did this happen? Where's your husband?"

"I don't know. California, probably. Alan . . . he wanted the best of everything, the best that money could buy. He got me started in this, then sold me to Lou. Alan is gone." Suzanne's shoulders shook as she cried. "He's gone for good this time."

"All right. Now. I'll get two tickets on the Denver Pacific to Evans. I'll buy a team and wagon there. We can be at home day after tomorrow." Then he remembered Lucky Lou's demands. "Well, we'll be

206

home soon. I'll need some help getting you out of here, but don't worry, I've got friends who'll help."

She sniffed, "Johnny, Johnny."

"Don't you worry. We're going home, Suzie. That's a promise. Listen, I'm gonna send a telegraph to Cheyenne. It'll take my friend a day or two to get here, but he'll get here. When he does, we're gonna take you out of this house. Understand? Promise me, Suzie, you'll hang on. Just hang on. Will you do that, Suzie? Promise me."

Her head moved, barely.

"Say it. Say you promise."

Voice weak, she said, "I promise."

"Remember what Poppa taught us—and Momma—that a man is only as good as his word? That goes for women, too. Keep thinking about home. You can get well. We'll get some chickens, and you can feed the chickens again. We can do the things we did as kids. Keep thinking about that. In a few days we'll be at home."

Her nod showed more life this time.

At the door, he looked back at her. "In just a little while. I'll be here again before you know it. Hang on, Suzie. Please."

At the telegraph office, Johnny sent a message to Bertram Goodfellow at Cheyenne, Territory of Wyoming. The message read, "Bert. Tell Jake I need his help. Fast. Great Northern. Urgent. Johnny."

Yes, he was told, it would be delivered soon. There were other telegrams ahead of his, but it would be delivered within two hours.

It hadn't taken Johnny long to decide he needed help. He could strap on the Dragoon and shoot it out with Lucky Lou's two bully boys, and maybe he'd even survive. But not if he had to carry Suzanne at the same time. No, he had to have help.

Come on, Jake.

He was at the depot the next evening, not expecting Jake to show up so soon, but hoping. He wasn't disappointed. He was flabbergasted.

Jake was the first to step down from the coach's iron steps to the iron stool and onto the cinder path. He was followed by Bert Goodfellow, and he was followed by—it couldn't be—Frankie.

Johnny gaped. Frankie sat her carpetbag down, ran to him, and wrapped her arms around his neck. "I had to come, Johnny. I just had to. You don't mind, do you?"

"No. Uh, what . . . ?" That was all Johnny could say.

"We got your wire," Bert answered. "You made it clear you needed help. It didn't say why or what kind of help, but we all came."

"Well, for . . ."

"Frankie was back in Cheyenne looking for you, and when I told her about the wire, she insisted on coming, too."

"Why, I, uh, boy, am I glad to see you-all." Johnny gave Frankie another hug, then turned to Bert. "How's your wound?"

"Well, I'm not going to run any footraces just yet, but I can get around all right."

Dark scowling Jake hefted a canvas duffel bag onto his left shoulder and asked, "What's the trouble down here, Johnny?"

"We have to find a place to talk. How about my hotel? We can't do anything until morning, anyway."

"Can you give us a hint?" Bert asked.

"I found my sister. She's sick and I have to get her home. We might have to do some shooting to get her out of the, uh, house."

"Oh, well, is that all?" Jake shrugged, "I thought we was gonna get to bust you out of jail, or somethin' excitin' like that."

They all rented rooms at the Great Northern, using bogus names. Jake and Bert shared a room. Johnny and Frankie had separate rooms. At supper, in a restaurant on Larimer Street, they sat at a table for four, and Johnny told them all about his sister, Lucky Lou, and the two hired gunslingers.

"Can she walk?" Bert asked.

"I don't know. Maybe a little bit. Not much. She's awful weak."

Frankie said, "That's where I come in."

"No, Frances, there might be some lead flying. We don't want you shot."

"Your sister needs a woman's help, Johnny. She'll have to get dressed, and she needs a woman to help with that. I can do things for her that a man can't."

Johnny mulled that over, looked at Jake, then at Bert, then back to Frankie. "I didn't think of that. You're right."

"I'm going in that house with you."

"All right, but we go in first."

"Well, now," Bert said, "let's give this some thought. You're planning to take her by rail to Evans and by wagon from there, is that right?"

"Yeah. That's the fastest way."

"The question, then, is do we just go in blasting, or do we try to get the drop on those two and avoid gunfire."

Scowling Jake said, "Let's go in shootin'. I hate

them kind of goons. It'd do me some good to eliminate a couple of 'em."

"I hate thieves," Bert said. "Her kind, that is."

"Let's tear the place up some. Give her somethin' to remember us by."

"Well now, Jake, uh, Johnny, do you think she's paying off the police?"

"She has to be."

"Then, when the fracus starts she might send someone running to the police. If that happens, we need to get out of there as soon as possible."

"Yeah," Johnny agreed, "otherwise we might be shooting it out with the whole Denver police department."

"That wouldn't surprise me at all," Bert said. "Judging from what I've seen of the police, they'd rather protect someone who's paying them under the table than do their job, like making the streets safe."

"I've got my sixteen-gauge in my warbag, and a box of shells. Them *po*-lice will pay a hell of a high price, and I don't think they'll wanta do that."

"Still," Bert argued, "it would be better to do this job as quickly and quietly as we can."

Their conversation was interrupted by a young waiter, who somehow managed to carry four platters of food at a time, one in each hand and one on each forearm.

"If I tried that," Bert commented, "I'd have food all over the floor."

"There's tricks to ever' trade," Jake allowed.

"I tried waitressing once," Frankie said. "I couldn't do it."

"Good pork." Bert chewed a mouthful.

Conversation was light until the meal was finished. Only Jake cleaned his platter. Johnny was too worried to eat much, Frankie was a light eater at all times, and Bert said he didn't need to gain any weight.

"Now then, Johnny, you've been thinking about this. What's your suggestion?"

"Best I can figure is to catch them by surprise. You and Jake stay out of sight, but near the door. I wasn't planning on Frances, but now that she's here, I think it would be best if her and me went in together. I'll tell that woman, Lucky Lou, that Frances is with me to help Suzie."

"And," Jake scowled, "we're s'posed to just stand outside and wait?"

"Yeah. Frances and I'll go up the stairs, and do what we can to get Suzie ready to travel. The two goons will try to stop us. I'll holler. That's when you two come in fast."

"Hmm. Sounds all right to me. What do you think, Jake?"

"Wal, mebbe that way we c'n catch 'em with their britches down—uh, pardon me, Frankie, I mean catch 'em by surprise."

"If we can do that, get the drop on them, we'll be out of there without firing a shot."

Frankie chuckled, "Oh, won't that madam be mad."

Chuckling with her, Bert said, "She'll be so mad she might bite herself."

"I'll tell you," Johnny said, serious now, "I swore I'd never hit a woman, but if she tries to keep me from saving my sister, I'll treat her like I would a man."

"I've got an extra pistol, a little .38, the one a fancy dan stuck in your face, Johnny. I can give it to Frankie."

"Oh no, Jake." Frankie said quickly. "I've never shot a gun in my life. I'm afraid of guns."

"All right, now," Johnny said, "the first thing I—Frances and I—have to do is get inside. The train pulls out at six o'clock, and there won't be anybody up in that house. There's some glass in the front door. I'll need something to break the glass so I can reach inside and unlock the door."

"And we have to have a carriage, one with two seats and a two-horse team. We have to have it ready to haul us to the depot in a hurry."

"We have to time it just right."

They talked on until they had it planned to the last detail they could think of, then agreed to meet in the hotel lobby at four A.M.

"Seldom," Bert said, "do things work exactly the way they're planned, but I think we've done the best we can."

"Four o'clock it is."

"Yep. That's when the party begins."

Chapter Twenty-four

In his room, Johnny washed his face, combed his hair, then went down the hall and knocked on Frankie's door. She was waiting for him, and opened the door immediately. Shutting the door behind him, he took her in his arms.

"I didn't get a chance in front of Bert and Jake," he murmured in her hair, "to tell you how happy I am you came back."

"I had to come back, Johnny. It was grand to see my folks and my brothers, but all I could think about was you. Johnny, I'm not going to rejoin my troupe. I want to go with you."

"I'm taking my sister home, to the farm. You said . . ."

She put a finger to his lips. "I know I said I was through with the farm life, but I'll go anywhere. I can cook, milk a cow, harness a team, pluck a chicken. I can do anything. You'll see."

"Milking cows ain't much like performing on a stage."

"I'll tell you what I'm through with, I'm through with indecent performances. I'm through with being leered at, pointed at, and whispered about, scared to death that my folks will find out what I'm doing. And I'm through with living out of a suitcase in hotel rooms. I'm through with actors who can't be trusted, whose word means nothing."

"The farm life is pretty dull, you know. Dull and hard. I'm not so sure I want to stay on the farm forever. We can sell it, Suzie and me. But I want to stay through the winter and give Suzie a chance to get well."

"Then you have all next winter to decide where you want to go and what you want to do. I don't care, just so I go, too."

The thought of spending time at the farm brought back an old worry: the Nash bunch. Please, he begged silently, if there is a god, let Him keep them off me until Suzie gets well and can take care of herself.

"Something wrong, Johnny?"

"Oh." He realized he'd been silent, frowning. "I, uh, it's nothing to do with you. I'm not going back to gambling. I don't know what I want to do, maybe get into a business of some kind, but like you said, I've got all winter to think about it. And I've got the money."

Stepping back, looking him squarely in the face, Frankie said, "Where you go, I go. Any argument?"

"None," he grinned. "None a-tall."

At four A.M., before daylight, they were gathered in the lobby of the Great Northern Hotel. The night clerk was sitting in a rocking chair, mouth open, head tilted back so far that Bert commented, "It's a wonder he doesn't break his neck."

Jake said, "I know a place down the street that's open all night. We can grab some grub in there."

It was a long room with no tables, just a counter. Again, only Jake cleaned his platter. He scowled at Bert's plate and asked, "You gonna eat that bread?"

"No. Here."

Just as the sun showed itself on the eastern horizon, they walked to the Denver Pacific depot, carrying their satchels, Bert carrying the canvas duffel bag he used for luggage. The three men wore six-guns in holsters. Yep, they were told, Old Number Eighteen was going to leave at six o'clock sharp. "That's her setting out there now," the station master said. "She's buildin' up steam, and she'll be rarin' to go." They bought five tickets to Cheyenne.

Their next chore was to find a cab. There was none on the street at that time of morning. Bert pulled his watch from a vest pocket, snapped open the cover, and said, "We're cutting it close."

"I'll fetch one," Jake said. "There's a livery a couple blocks from here. Be right back." He took off at a fast walk, trotting at times, holding down the big pistol on his right hip.

Johnny walked in a circle, studying the ground until he found a brick. "This oughta do," he said.

Again, Bert looked at his watch. "Come on, Jake."

Jake came, riding in a carriage pulled by a matched team of gray horses. "Climb in, folks." They entered, sat facing each other. "I caught 'im throwin' the harness on," Jake said. "Promised 'im a pile of money to do what we want."

"Good. Now, it's a quarter after five," Bert said, looking at his watch again. "It's going to be close, but that's what we want. Johnny, tell him where to go."

At 5:25, they were in front of Lucky Lou's. As they got out, Jake pulled his double-barreled shotgun from the duffel bag. Johnny checked the loads in the Dragoon. Bert's pistol fired metallic cartridges, and he flipped open the cylinder to be sure it was loaded.

The coach driver gaped at them. "Hey, you fellers . . . what's goin' on?"

Bert fished a gold coin out of his pocket and handed it up to him. "Here's ten dollars. There's another ten in it for you if you wait here for us. In fact, I'll make it a double eagle. No matter what happens, you wait here and be ready to run for the depot. All right."

The driver was hesitant, "Well, uh, I dunno."

"Here." Bert handed him another gold coin. "There's twenty bucks more if you're here when we come out. You're in no danger at all, and we're not going to rob anyone or anything like that. We're going to rescue a woman from in there. Just wait here—will you?"

With a gulp and a bobbing of his Adam's apple, the driver nodded in agreement.

In a group they climbed two steps and stood in front of the door. Johnny hefted his brick, then smashed the etched-glass door pane. In the early morning quiet, the breaking glass sounded like a small explosion. Reaching through, Johnny groped for the inside latch. He swore, "Damn it, there's no latch. The damned door is locked from the inside and there's no key."

"The window, then."

More glass was smashed. The big bay window was

built in squares, and Johnny broke all the glass out of a bottom square. Dropping the brick, he quickly crawled inside and pushed a heavy drape out of the way, letting in a dim light. Frankie followed him, ripping her dress on a shard of glass. Johnny whispered, "They're all awake by now. Let's get up those stairs fast."

She looked around until she spotted the stairs in the dim light. "I see them. I'm right behind you."

There was no use trying to be quiet. Johnny took the stairs two at a time, getting ahead of Frankie. At the door to Suzanne's room, he waited for her, then opened the door and stepped inside.

The room was dark until he threw open the drapes and let daylight in. Suzanne was lying on her side, eyes closed. Johnny shook her. "Suzie, it's me. It's time to go."

"What? Huh?" Suzanne's eyes popped open.

Frankie sat on the bed beside her, took her hand, "My name is Frances. Most folks call me Frankie. I'm a friend of Johnny's, and I'm here to help you. We have to hurry. Can you stand up?"

"Huh? What?"

Johnny yanked open a closet door and threw out two dresses and a pair of shoes. Frankie pulled the bed covers down and dragged Suzanne's feet off the bed. "Can you stand up? We have to hurry."

"Why, uh, my gosh."

"We must hurry." She pulled the sick woman to her feet. Suzanne was wearing a long nightdress and nothing else. Frankie grabbed a plain dark dress, glanced at Johnny, and said, "Turn your head, will you."

Footsteps were coming up the stairs. Heavy footsteps.

Johnny ran down the hall to the head of the stairs. Lucky Lou was in the lead, holding her long gown up as she climbed. The two bouncers were behind her. One was buttoning his suspenders. The other was buckling on his gun belt.

Drawing the Colt Dragoon, Johnny fired a shot over their heads. The explosion reverberated throughout the house. Smoke and fire belched from the gun. The madam and her two goons stopped, stared. Then the woman screamed: "Get 'im. Get 'im, God damn it."

They clawed for their guns. Johnny dropped to the floor to make a smaller target of himself. The Dragoon boomed again. Glancing behind him, Johnny saw Frankie peering around the door of Suzanne's room. He motioned for her to stay back. A lead slug slammed into the wall at the end of the hall. Another tore a hole in the ceiling. Johnny fired again.

Outside, Bert and Jake heard the shots and knew it was time to go in. Jake went through the window first, the shotgun in his hands. He hit the floor on his shoulder, rolled to his knees.

One of the bouncers saw him, snapped a shot in his direction. The sixteen-gauge roared, and a stair step shattered under the bouncer's feet, sending him staggering back.

Lucky Lou screamed, "Get 'em. Get the sons-of-bitches. God damn it, shoot the bastards."

For the moment, the hired guns were trained on Jake and Bert. Exploding cartridges filled the house with thunder. Acrid gunsmoke was thick on the stairs and in the parlour. While he had a chance, Johnny scrambled to his feet and ran back to Suzanne's room. She was standing as Frankie finished slipping a long dress over her head. Her eyes were weak, but her strained expression and clenched jaws showed she was trying to stay upright. Frankie knelt, got the dress pulled down to her ankles, then ordered her to sit. Johnny went to the door to stand guard.

Gunfire ceased for a few seconds, but not Lucky Lou's screams. "God damn it, kill the bastards. Kill the sons-of-bitches. Kill 'em, God damn it."

Looking back, Johnny saw his sister sitting on the edge of the bed while Frankie, kneeling on the floor, forced her feet into a pair of low shoes. Frankie stood, pulled the sick woman to her feet.

"Can we go now, Johnny?"

Johnny took another look toward the stairs, then ducked back when he saw a gun aimed at him. The bullet knocked splinters off the edge of the door. "One second," Johnny yelled.

He stepped out to where he could return the fire, but found he wasn't needed. From where he was, he saw Bert coming up the stairs, holding his sixgun at eye level ahead of him. Saw one of the hired goons turn toward him. Saw smoke shoot out of Bert's gun. Saw it recoil. Saw the goon grab his right shoulder, spin half-around and fall to his knees.

"All right," Johnny yelled at Frankie, "let's go."

"We need help, Johnny."

Suzanne was on her feet, but her knees were trying to buckle under her. Only Frankie's shoulder under her left arm was holding her up. Holstering the Dragoon, Johnny hurried to his sister's right side, got her right arm over his left shoulder.

"All right, Suzie? We're leaving now."

Between the two of them, they half-carried, half-dragged the sick woman to the door. Grimacing with determination, Suzanne managed to move her feet a little. "I-I'm all right," she said through tight jaws. "I'm all right."

"Sure you are." Frankie's voice was calm. "Johnny told me about you, Suzanne. You're no quitter."

Through the door they went, slowly, out into the hall. Lucky Lou saw them and yelled, "There they are! Kill 'em. Don't let 'em get away. Kill 'em, God damn it!"

The goon on his knees at the head of the stairs raised his gun. In a half-second Johnny had his thumb on the Dragoon's hammer, had it out of its holster, leveled. The big pistol boomed. Flame and smoke belched. The goon fell face down, his gun slipping from his fingers.

Lucky Lou screamed, "God damn it, God damn it."

Downstairs, Jake held his shotgun waist high, wishing Bert would step aside and give him a shot. The second hired gunslinger was four steps above Bert. He whirled, gun ready. Bert pulled the trigger on his pistol.

The metallic rimfire cartridge failed to explode. Worse, the cartridge was jammed in so the cylinder wouldn't turn.

While Bert tried desperately to turn the cylinder and get another cartridge in line with the barrel, the hired goon grinned an evil grin and took aim at his chest.

Jake yelled, "Bert! Drop!"

Bert jumped aside. The sixteen-gauge roared. A full load of buckshot caught the goon squarely in the middle. He folded at the waist and pitched forward, turning somersalts down the stairs.

Lucky Lou screamed, "God damn it, God damn it."

"Shut up," Bert said. "Shut your fat face. Johnny?"

"We're coming," Johnny said.

Suzanne was shuffling her feet forward, but was unable to stand by herself. With Frankie on one side and Johnny on the other, they got her to the top of the stairs. Jake put his shotgun down and came up the stairs to help.

Bert had Lucky Lou by the shoulders, shaking her. "Where's the key to the front door?"

"Go to hell, you bastards. You God-damned sons-of-bitches."

Shaking her again, Bert said, "Where is it?"

When she screamed another obscenity, Bert grabbed the front of her gown and pulled her to the top of the stairs. He waited until his partners were at the bottom, stepping around a dead man, then gave the madam a hard shove. Lucky Lou went down the stairs a lot faster then she had ever come up them. Jake let her fall on top of her dead hireling, then he, too, grabbed the front of her gown and hauled her to her feet.

Screaming obscenities, she clawed at Jake's face. He grabbed her by the hair with one hand, held her head back, and ripped open the top of her gown with the other.

The key was hanging from a silver chain around her neck.

Jake gave it a jerk, but the chain refused to break. "Bend your head down or I'll yank your damn head off with it."

"Go to hell, you bastards. Rot in hell, God damn you."

It was Bert, coming up behind Lucky Lou, who forced her head down. Jake pulled the chain over her hair, mussing the blond hairdo. He hurried to the door and unlocked it.

"God damn you all! God damn you all to hell!"

"The cab's still there," Jake said, picking up his shotgun. He broke the gun down and reloaded both barrels. Then he snapped it together again and shoved the twin bores into Lucky Lou's stomach. "You've prob'ly got more guns in the house, but I'll tell you somethin', woman—if I see you with a gun, this here Rocky Mountain howitzer'll blast you in two! Get it?"

Lucky Lou quit screaming. Suddenly, her mouth was clamped shut, and her eyes were fixed on the shotgun. Slowly, Jake raised the bores until they were only inches from her face. "Know what one blast can do to that fat face? You won't have a face. They'll be scrubbing pieces of your brains off the walls. Get it?"

Her mouth opened, her lips trembled, but no words came out.

Frankie said, "Wait a minute." She ran up the stairs, and in twenty seconds was back, carrying a heavy quilt and a thick pillow. "Suzie will need this."

Bert held the door wide open. With a bow and a smile, he said, "We're leaving now, madam. Believe me, it was a pleasure."

Chapter Twenty-five

Bert was the last to enter the carriage. Before he got in, he snapped open his watch. "We've got four minutes." He handed the driver another gold coin, a twenty-dollar double eagle. "Can these horses run?"

Reaching for the coin, examining it, the driver answered, "Yessir."

"Get us to the Denver Pacific depot—*fast*."

He didn't get both feet inside before the driver yelled, "Heeyup," and snapped a long buggy whip over the horses' backs. Helping hands grabbed Bert by the shoulders and pulled him inside as the coach lurched forward. The horses broke into a trot, then a gallop. Within seconds, the team and carriage were racing down the street, the buggy whip popping.

They heard the locomotive's whistle. It whistled again. The big black thirty-ton engine was ready to go. Bert growled, "Don't you dare leave early. Don't you dare."

Then the driver was yelling, "Whoa. Whoa now." And they were there.

Old No. Eighteen was hissing and steaming, like a giant animal eager to run. The conductor was standing by his iron step in front of a coach door, looking at his watch. He hollered, " 'Bo-o-ard." He reached down to pick up the step, when Bert called out, "Hold on. Hold on there. We're coming. We've got a sick woman here."

The two gray horses were blowing hard through fluted nostrils, sides heaving. Bert said to the driver, "Thanks, mister. You can let these animals rest now."

Grinning, the driver said, "I made 'er, didn't I?"

Johnny and Frankie helped Suzanne out of the carriage while Bert hurried to the conductor, ready to detain him by force, if necessary. Jake had his shotgun back inside the duffel bag. He carried all their luggage, even the quilt and pillow.

"How sick is she?" the conductor asked, eyeing Suzanne's shuffling feet and pale face.

"She's sick," Frankie answered. "That's all I can say."

"We ain't got no sleeping car."

"We'll manage."

They got Suzanne up the steps. She tried to walk, did the best she could, her face screwed up with determination. Frankie took the quilt from Jake, folded it, and placed it carefully on a seat. "This won't be so hard to sit on," she said. Then they lowered the sick woman to the seat, next to the window, a pillow behind her head. Frankie sat next to her. "Lean on me. You can lie down and put your head on my lap if you want to."

224

"Thank you," the sick woman said weakly. "I'm sorry to be so . . ."

"Never mind that," Frankie said quickly. "We all need help sometimes."

Johnny sat next to Frankie, wishing he could do more to help his sister.

Outside, the conductor waved a signal to the engineer, and the train started moving, slowly at first, jerking cars all down the line. The big engine puffed smoke out of its diamond stack, and gradually it picked up speed.

Johnny let out a sigh of relief. Bert said, "Looks like we accomplished everything." Jake, sitting across the aisle next to Bert, said dryly, "Next time you want us, Johnny, find somethin' excitin' to do, will you?"

Soon they were out of the city, watching the hills and trees roll past. The coach swayed and shook. Suzanne tried to sit up, but her pinched face told Frankie she was very uncomfortable. "Here." Frankie placed the pillow on her lap, and scooted toward the aisle. Johnny stood to give them more room, and hung onto the seat backs to keep his balance. "Just lay your head on my lap," Frankie murmured. Suzanne lay her head on the pillow, folded her legs, and got her feet on the seat. Tears filled her eyes.

"I-I'm not worth all you've done. I'm so ashamed!"

"Don't be." Frankie stroked her hair. "I've done things I'm not proud of. I know how it can happen. When you get better, we'll have a lot to talk about, you and me."

"Thank you." The sick woman's eyes closed. Her

brother was here, watching over her. And she had a new friend.

Up front, the fireman worked hard shoveling coal into the engine's firebox. Heat in the fire compartment was enough to melt steel, but the fireman wore no protection. He scooped up a shovelful of coal, then with one hand pulled a chain that opened the firebox door, and quickly threw the shovelful inside before releasing the chain and slamming the door. A steam gauge showed the pressure in the boiler at 130 pounds.

The country rolled past.

"She needs food," Frankie said, stroking Suzanne's hair. "I'll bet she hasn't eaten anything in a long time. I'll bet that awful woman didn't fix anything a sick person can eat."

"Probably not," Johnny said. "What do you think she can eat?"

"Soup. Something that goes down easy, but has some strength in it. My mother used to make soup from beef stock. And she fed us kids a lot of milk when we were sick. That's what she needs, Johnny. When we get to . . . wherever we're going, I'll need some beef and milk. Can we get that?"

"We can get anything we need at Rollinsville. Only, I wish we had something for her sooner. Maybe that café at Evans will have something."

"They ought to."

Long before noon, the train began slowing on its approach to Evans. "Here's where we get off," Johnny said. "I'll buy a team and wagon, and we can be in Rollinsville in two hours and home in another hour. Bert, you and Jake going on to Cheyenne?"

"Yep. Got a business to run. Jake here, he's got money he ain't spent yet. Listen, Johnny, they might—what with the telegraph and all—the police in Denver might send a message to Sheriff Rathke, but nobody in Denver knows our names. We gave fake names at the hotel. I don't know everything about the law, but it seems to me they ought to have names on arrest warrants. In any case, we won't mention your name."

"I've thought of that," Johnny said. "They won't have any trouble finding the carriage driver, and when they do, they'll know which way we went. But only Lucky Lou can identify us, and I don't think she'll go to Cheyenne to do that."

"No. What's done is done, and if she's smart, she'll just forget about it."

"The way you two talk," Frankie said, "a body'd think you were old hands at running from the law."

Johnny and Bert looked at her, then at each other. They grinned. Jake scowled.

Everyone got out of the passenger coach at Evans, everyone except Frankie and Suzanne. "I don't want to move her till you find a place for her to lie down," Frankie said. "And she needs food."

"I'll go in and see about something to eat," Bert said. "Johnny, you can go do your horse trading."

In a weak voice, Suzanne said, "I can walk. I think I can." She forced herself upright, but her face was white and she looked ready to collapse.

"Don't try to walk, Suzie," Johnny said. "Stay here till I get a wagon."

He found Hutchison in his trashy office in a corner of the barn, writing in a ledger with a lead pencil. Hutchison looked up when Johnny's shadow fell across his scarred rolltop desk. A spring chair creaked as he leaned back in it. "See you're still among the livin'. Come to buy?"

"Maybe." Johnny didn't want to appear too eager. "Let's see what you've got in the way of a light wagon."

The lean, stringy Hutchison led him behind the barn to where a half-dozen freight wagons with big wheels were lined up. "I don't need anything that big."

"Got a buckboard over here. She's got a spring seat and new runnin' gear."

"Let's see it."

The buckboard was parked behind the freight wagons. The shallow bed had seen a lot of use and was splintery. The sideboards were also split and splintery. The tailgate was missing. The seat was mounted high on leaf springs, and looked to be strong enough. Many pairs of boot heels, resting on the dashboard, had worn it smooth. Johnny squatted and looked under the wagon. The front axle had no fifth wheel. All that kept it from wearing out when it turned under the bolster were two pieces of strap iron. The axle, tongue, doubletree, and singletrees looked to be in good shape.

"She's been over the road," Hutchison said, scratching a two-day growth of whiskers, "and lots of places where there ain't no road, but like I said, she's got a nearly new runnin' gear. All the important parts is good as new."

"How much?"

"Seventy-five."

"Aw, come on, now."

"What'll you offer?"

"No more than fifty."

"Make it sixty."

"It takes horses to pull a wagon. What have you got to sell?"

"Over here."

Johnny followed him.

"Them two." Hutchison pointed at a bay and a brown munching hay out of a wooden rack. They were in a pen with Johnny's bay saddle horse and four bigger horses. "You can ride 'em or work 'em in harness. They're plumb gentle."

The horses weighed around twelve hundred and fifty pounds each and were well matched. "How old are they?"

"The bay's nine and the brown horse is comin' eight. They been workin' together for three years. They're sound and healthy. I'll guarantee it."

"What are you asking?"

"Hunnerd and fifty for the pair."

"That's too much. A hundred."

"Hunnerd and fifty. That's with a good set of harness."

Johnny knew he ought to dicker more, but he didn't have time. "If the harness is strong, it's a deal," he said. "Now, you wouldn't happen to have a cot of some kind? I've got a sick woman with me."

"Happens I do. It's a canvas cot with no springs or nothin', but some a my teamsters've been more'n happy to catch some winks on it. Seldom use it anymore, though."

"How much?"

"Oh, make it five bucks."

"Put it in the wagon, will you, and hitch up the team. I'll pay you in U.S. greenbacks."

"Wanta pay me now?"

"I haven't seen the horses move yet, and I haven't seen the harness. If everything's good, I'll pay you on the spot, and I'll pay you for feeding my saddle horse."

"Deal."

Suzanne was sitting up and eating out of a china bowl. "It's beef stew," Frankie said, "but she's chewing a little of it, and swallowing the gravy. Bert said the only milk they have here is in those cans."

"That won't do, huh?"

"It'll do to cook with, I guess, but it won't take the place of fresh milk and butter."

"I'll buy a cow as soon as I can."

The sick woman's hand was shaky, but she managed to get a spoon to her mouth. She swallowed with a gulp. "This is . . . this is good. Wish I could eat more, but I don't, uh, I'm afraid my stomach . . ."

"Just eat what you can, Suzanne. Johnny calls you Suzie. What would you like for me to call you?"

A weak smile touched the sick woman's face. "After what's happened . . . anything you want."

"Suzie, then."

"I bought a team and wagon. They'll be hitched up and ready in a minute, and there'll be a canvas cot in the wagon. We can be at home in a few hours."

"Bert said they sell groceries in one end of that railroad coach they use for a restaurant. Maybe I can buy enough to last a day or two, and you can buy some more later. That way we won't have to stop. I want to get Suzie to bed as quick as we can."

"That's a good plan. Here, here's some money." Johnny had to reach inside his shirt and unbutton a pocket of his money belt. But Frankie said, "I've got some money. First, though, Johnny, Suzie is embarrassed, but it can't be helped. We have to take her to the toilet."

"Oh. Sure. When?"

"Now. It's over there behind the restaurant, not far from that house."

By then the coach was filling with passengers again. Bert got on board and volunteered to return the stew bowl and spoon. "The conductor said she'll be pulling out in five minutes, Johnny. Can I do anything else?"

"Don't know of anything. We sure do thank you, Bert. You and Jake. I couldn't have done it by myself."

"Come for a visit when you get a chance, and meanwhile, take care of this lady here." Bert leaned forward, his face close to Suzanne's. "I wish you the best, ma'am. Johnny has talked a lot about you, and no matter what's happened, you're a lady. You're a real lady."

"Thank you, Mr. Goodfellow." Tears welled up in Suzanne's eyes. "You've all been so wonderful. I wish . . . the only thing I can do now is say thank you."

"That's good enough for me. Come and visit when you can." His eyes swept over Johnny and Frankie. "All of you. I'll be tickled pink to see you."

"It's time to get off," Johnny said. "Here, Suzie, let me take one arm. Frances will take the other."

"I'll bring your luggage and stuff," Bert volunteered.

"See that buckboard over by the barn? I just bought it. Put everything in there."

"I'll do it."

"Bo-o-a-rd," the conductor yelled.

With Johnny on one side and Frankie on the other, they got Suzanne down the steps. Suzanne could only shuffle her feet. "We won't be getting back on," Johnny said to the conductor. "We live not far from here."

"You won't? You bought tickets to Cheyenne."

"Yeah." Johnny didn't explain, just left the conductor frowning, puzzled.

Jake didn't like goodbyes nor thank-yous, and he

stood off to one side, his fingers in his hip pockets, a scowl on his face. Johnny waved. He lifted one hand in return.

The little narrow outhouse with a half-moon cut in the door stood a hundred feet from the frame house. Freshly washed clothes were hanging on a line between the two buildings. The door to the outhouse was closed, and they had to wait until a woman came out. When she saw Johnny, she started to say something scolding, but changed her mind when she noticed Suzanne.

"Now," Frankie said, "Suzie can lean against the wall inside. We won't need you for now, Johnny."

"I'll get the wagon." He went back to the pens and saddled his bay horse, tied him with a strong halter to the back of the wagon while Hutchison watched. The harness had been repaired in places, but the repairs seemed to have been done with expertise. "Let's see, Mr. Hutchison, I owe you, umm, two hundred and twenty U.S. greenback dollars, including five for feeding my horse. Right?"

"That agrees with my calc'lations."

Reaching inside his shirt to his moneybelt, Johnny pulled out a handful of bills. He counted the correct amount and stuffed the rest in his pants pocket. "You guaranteed the team to be sound."

"I did, and I'll back up my guarantee. They ain't shod, as you've no doubt seen for yourself, but the roads around here ain't hard, and they can go a long ways barefooted."

"Where we live, folks don't usually shoe their horses."

"I gen'ly do, but them two ain't been used for a while."

Two satchels, Johnny's and Frankie's, were in the bed of the wagon, and the quilt and pillow had been

232

piled on top of an Army surplus cot. The two horses tossed their heads, but didn't try to move when the locomotive whistle tooted twice. "They're used to that," Hutchison said. "They're used to most ever'thing short of cannon fire. They ain't had to put up with that yet."

The locomotive puffed black smoke from its stack, spun its six big drive wheels, and chug-chugged away from Evans, jerking its string of cars along behind it.

Johnny climbed to the buckboard seat, gathered the driving lines, clucked to the team, and drove the wagon close to the outhouse. When the door opened, he got down and helped lift Suzanne to a sitting position on the end of the wagon bed. Then he climbed back up and helped her onto the cot.

"It's not as comfortable as your bed at home, but it's no worse than the railroad coach."

Frankie said, "Wait here, Johnny, and I'll go see what groceries I can buy."

While he waited, Johnny managed to straighten the quilt under his sister and get the pillow in a better position under her head. "I should have done this before you got up here, Suzie," he said. "I wasn't thinking."

Hutchison said, "Lookee yonder." He was pointing to the northeast.

Looking in that direction, Johnny saw horses coming, a herd of horses. He counted five riders with the herd. When they came closer, he noticed that the horses were all saddle horse size, and most had small white saddle marks high on their withers.

"Must be some cow outfit's remuda," Hutchison allowed, "headin' back to Texas."

"Must be." But when they came closer still, there was something about one of the riders that pulled at Johnny's mind. The man was big, with a hawk nose that had been broken. He looked mean. Another man was short, with a pug nose and thick lips.

Johnny's legs suddenly went weak. His throat tightened. He gasped, "Oh, no. Not now. Oh, Lord, not now."

The big one was Powell Nash. The short one was Court Nash.

Chapter Twenty-Six

While Johnny and Hutchison watched, the riders gathered the herd east of the barn and corrals, then two of them split off and headed their way. "Got anything to eat here?" one of them yelled.

"Yup." Hutchison pointed to the converted railroad coach.

Johnny went to the other side of the buckboard team and, keeping his head down, pretended to adjust the harness on the nigh horse.

"Like to dicker," Powell Nash said, riding up. "We ran out of money a while back, but we've got some damned good horses here. How about we sell you a couple good horses?"

Hutchison replied, "I'm sellin' horses myownself."

"You can take your pick. Cheap. All we need is some eatin' money."

"Where you comin' from?"

"Wyomin' Territory. We're the hashknife outfit goin' back south."

"Got a bill of sale?"

"For all 'em? Naw. There's forty-two horses over there. But I'll write you out a bill of sale if you want."

"What're you askin'?"

"I said cheap. Make it thirty-five a head. You can take your pick."

Hutchison had to think it over. He was trying to get rid of some horses himself, but if he could buy horses cheap enough, he could make a profit. "Twenty-five."

"Like I said, we're out of cash, so if you'll give me fifty bucks, you can go pick out two."

Hutchison didn't know it, but he was buying stolen horses. Johnny knew it. He wanted to warn him, but he didn't. He couldn't. If he showed his face, there would be a fight, and with Suzanne sick in the back of the wagon, he couldn't fight. He had to keep his face hidden and his mouth shut.

Unless he could get Hutchison away from the two gunsels.

The stage and freight owner counted out fifty dollars from the money Johnny had just given him. Powell Nash dismounted. "You can ride my horse over there and look 'em over. My boys'll rope out the two you want." He pocketed the money. "I'm gonna get some chuck. You comin', Court?"

"Yeah, we'll eat and go spell the other boys while they eat." Court Nash too dismounted, and walked, leading his horse to a hitchrail in front of the barn. They passed Frankie, who was coming from the store carrying a cloth bag half-full of groceries. Hutchison mounted the big man's horse.

Speaking low, Johnny said, "Wait a minute."

Hutchison paused, a questioning look on his face. Johnny watched out of the corner of his eyes until the two Nashes went into the café, then said, "You bought stolen horses. I'd bet on it. Those two fit the descriptions of two men who shot and robbed a merchant in Cheyenne. They're the Nash boys. You've heard of the Nash gang?"'"

"Aw, for . . . I shoulda knowed. Now what? I gotta git my money back."

"You'd better have a gun in your hand when you ask for it. Those two are killers."

"Aw, for . . ."

"I'd help you, but I've got a sick woman here."

"It ain't your loss. I dunno. I reckon I might as well cut out two horses and wait for the law to catch up. Looks like it's that, or get in a gunfight with five horse thieves."

"The odds are on their side."

"Well." Hutchison frowned at the ground, thinking. He looked up at Johnny. "You ain't positive they're stole, you're just thinkin' they might be."

"I'd bet anything they were stolen. I know those two."

"Well, just in case they ain't, I'm gonna cut out a couple of 'em. I'll make sure I get a bill of sale in writin'."

Johnny shrugged as if to say it wasn't his business. Hutchison turned the horse around and rode at a walk around the barn toward the herd. Johnny wanted to do something, but he didn't know what to do. Looking back, he saw Suzanne's eyes half-closed and Frankie sitting on a satchel next to the cot.

"It's no concern of ours, is it Johnny."

"Naw. Well, those two are the ones that shot Bert. I hate to see them get away."

"But we have to go."

Shaking his head sadly, Johnny said, "Yeah, you're right. We have to go." Glancing fearfully back at the café, he clucked to the team.

As the wagon moved, Johnny's eyes checked all the wheels to see if they turned straight without wobbling. They did. He looked ahead again just as the team and wagon turned a corner around a big corral. That was when he saw another rider. This one was coming from the northeast, too, but suddenly reined up. The three riders with the herd saw him. A gun fired.

The latecomer turned his horse west, and spurred hard toward the barn. More guns fired. Suddenly the horse went down, pitching the rider over its head. The rider scrambled to his feet, and, bending low, ran for a shallow draw just east of the barn. Bullets followed him, forcing him to hit the ground flat on his belly in the draw.

That rider also looked familiar to Johnny.

"Oh, no," Johnny groaned.

"Who is it, Johnny?" Frankie asked.

"I think that's Sheriff Rathke from Cheyenne, and they've got him afoot and pinned down."

"Sheriff Rathke?"

"Yeah. He's trailing a stolen herd of horses."

"Oh, my gosh."

The two Nash brothers were running out of the restaurant toward the barn, sixguns drawn. They paid no attention to Johnny. Hutchison had turned his mount around and was riding at a lope back to the barn, bending low over the horse's neck. Over in the draw, Sheriff Rathke got to his knees and fired two quick shots, then ducked as bullets thudded into the ground around him. Two of the riders with the herd rode at a gallop to the east, aiming to get around and behind the sheriff. The other was afoot, hanging onto the reins of a nervous horse and shooting at the sheriff.

Now the Nash brothers were on the other side of the barn, walking cautiously toward the draw, guns ready. Rathke would soon be in a crossfire from three directions. Worse, his attention was on the other gunmen, and he didn't see the two brothers coming.

Frankie was standing in the wagon, watching the gunfight, too. "Oh, my gosh—they're gonna kill him."

Handing the lines to Frankie, Johnny said, "I've got to do something."

"No, Johnny, you can't. Your sister . . . we have to go."

"I can't just watch the man get killed. Besides, if they kill the sheriff, they'll have nothing to lose by killing everybody. Hang onto these horses." He climbed down, using a front wheel hub as a step.

"Don't get yourself killed, Johnny."

The sick woman raised up on one elbow so she could see over the wagon sides. "What's going on? What's wrong."

"O-o-oh, Suzie," Frankie wailed, "everything's wrong."

Chapter Twenty-seven

Johnny Vorhes checked the loads in the Colt Dragoon, and began walking toward the sheriff. He was behind the two brothers, and he expected them to spot him, whirl, and shoot. Holding his gun straight out at eye level, he hoped to be able to shoot first. But they were so intent on getting within easy sixgun range of the man in the draw they didn't know anyone was behind them.

The sheriff was on his knees, reloading his gun. Still, he didn't see the two. The other gunman on foot fired a shot that kicked dirt in the sheriff's face, forcing him to duck lower, then he, too, had to reload. The big man and the short one were getting closer, ready to fire.

Johnny had an urge to yell a warning, but if he did, he would be a perfect target himself, walking where there was no cover. At least Rathke had his draw.

Gunfire had scattered the herd of stolen horses, and they were running and kicking up their heels, partly out of fear and partly for the fun of it.

Still, Rathke didn't see the two.

Powell Nash stopped, held a short-barreled pistol in both hands, and sighted down the barrel. He was close enough that he couldn't miss. Johnny took careful aim, too, and yelled, "Hey! Powell!" The big man looked back, whirled, and snapped a shot. The Dragoon bucked and popped. Powell Nash dropped to his knees, clutched his stomach with both hands, then rolled over onto his side in a fetal position. Court Nash spun on his heels, jabbed his gun in Johnny's direction, and squeezed the trigger. The lead ball missed by inches.

Johnny was close enough now that, in a glance, he saw the surprised look on the sheriff's face, saw the star pinned to his shirt. The sheriff fired at Court Nash. His bullet missed and whined past Johnny's head.

"Sheriff," Johnny yelled. "Sheriff, it's John Vorhes. I'm on your side." While he yelled, he turned his gun toward Court Nash.

Nash sputtered, "Vorhes, God damn you!" His gun boomed again, but again it was a scared, hasty shot. Glancing about, Nash discovered he was between two enemy guns, and his brother was down. He ran.

Both women in the buckboard heard the shooting. Frankie, from the high seat, could see over the corrals. She said to herself, "He's not hurt. Oh, please, God."

"What?" Suzanne pleaded. "What's going on?"

241

Turning her head, Frankie said, "I can see Johnny. He's not hurt. One man was shot, but Johnny's not hurt."

Hutchison rode the horse into the barn, out of sight. Soon, he came out of the near end of the barn on foot, carrying a pistol. But he came toward the buckboard, not out to the gunfight.

"Mr. Hutchison," Frankie yelled. "They're shooting each other over there."

Red-faced, Hutchison snapped, "I know. It ain't my fight. I got to protect my woman in the house."

"But, can't you . . . no, I guess you can't."

"You women ought to get out of that wagon and come to the house. It ain't safe out here."

"We can't. She can't walk."

"Well, mebbe I can . . ." He was close to the wagon when he saw Court Nash run around the corrals. The gunman ran to his horse tied to the hitchrail in front of the barn. While Hutchison and the women watched, he untied the horse and tried to mount. But gunfire had the horse dancing nervously, and Nash couldn't get his foot in the stirrup.

"Halt!" Hutchison yelled. "Stop right there. Stop or I'll shoot!" He had his gun raised, ready.

Court Nash gave up trying to get on the horse. He turned at Hutchison's warning, drew his gun. Both men fired at the same time.

Hutchison suddenly dropped his pistol and grabbed his right arm above the elbow. He spun half-around, but stayed on his feet. The short man again tried to get on his horse. This time, the horse reared and jerked the reins out of his hand. It took off running, reins flying.

The buckboard horses were also nervous at the gunfire, and were pulling on their bits, trying to bolt. "Whoa," Frankie said, forcing calmness into her voice. "Whoa, now." The horses quieted.

The outlaw eyed the buckboard and Johnny's saddle horse tied to it. He started toward it.

"Oh, my gosh," Frankie said. "Oh, no." She glanced back at the sick woman, still raised up on one elbow. She glanced at the sixgun Hutchison had dropped near the wagon wheel. She made a quick decision.

Hanging onto the lines with one hand, she climbed down from the wagon, stepping from the front wheel hub to the ground. She snatched up the gun, and climbed back to the seat.

"Hey," Nash yelled. "You. Get out of that wagon." He was coming, holding his gun ready. "Get out of there."

"Oh, my gosh," Frankie muttered. Hastily, she wrapped the lines around the brake handle, and, using both thumbs, cocked the pistol the way she'd seen the men do it.

But she made a mistake. She was pulling on the trigger at the same time she forced the hammer back. The gun boomed and jumped in her hands, sending a ball through the floor of the buckboard near her feet. Court Nash raised his gun, aimed at Frankie.

He fired just as the team bolted.

Johnny Vorhes yelled again, "Sheriff Rathke, it's John Vorhes. I'm on your side."

The gunman afoot had his sixgun reloaded now, and he swung it toward Johnny. Johnny knew he was a good target out in the open, and when he saw the gun swing his way, he dived to the ground and rolled. He tried to shoot, but the gunman kept his horse between them. Johnny jumped up and ran for cover. A bullet kicked up dirt just in front of him and another right behind him.

"Vorhes," the sheriff barked as Johnny slid on his belly into the draw. "What in tarnation you doin' here?"

"Oh," Johnny said, rolling onto his back, forcing a drawl into his voice, "I just happened to be here. Looks like you got trouble, sheriff."

"Yeah, sure. I always got trouble."

"There's shooters on three sides of us. Which side do you want to watch?"

"Nobody asked you for help."

"You never wanted my help, but I'm here, and I'm in this fight whether you like it or not."

"Well, I reckon two guns're better'n one."

"Sure." A shade of bitterness crept into Johnny's voice. "Even a tinhorn gambler's gun. But," he added, "I ain't got my powder flask with me, and I've got maybe four shots left."

"Well, don't shoot unless you got a good target."

"I'm sure glad you told me that, Sheriff. I'd have shot off in all damned directions if you wasn't here to advise me."

"You gettin' sarcastic, Vorhes?"

"I'm always sarcastic where the law is concerned."

"You oughta do some thinkin' about that."

Keeping watch to the north, where he expected the two riders to show up, Johnny asked, "How do you get into these jackpots? How come you're trailing five horse thieves by yourself? Won't the county hire a deputy?"

"No. This bunch killed two Texas cowboys and wounded two more. The cowman that owns the horses has already gone back to Texas."

"Well, what made you think you could catch five gunhands by yourself?"

"I had to try."

"Why?"

"Because somebody has to. If we're ever gonna have law and order, somebody has to try."

"The law doesn't seem to be working too good."

"It will. If we give it a chance, maybe we can get the kinks out of it and make it work."

Glancing back at the sheriff, Johnny said, "Sure. It's up to the politicians to make the laws, and while they're sitting around with their thumbs up their asses and fleecing the taxpayers, you're out here dodging lead."

"The law won't work if it ain't enforced."

Johnny said no more for the moment.

"You asked some questions, Vorhes, now answer me one: I allus figured you as a man that has no respect for the law, yet this is the second time I've knowed you to side with the law. How come?"

"There's more to this fight than stolen horses," Johnny answered. A half-smile turned up one corner of his mouth. "Besides, like I said before, I don't like the odds." His smile vanished when he heard gunfire coming from the other side of the barn. "Oh-oh. The women are over there. If anything happens to them, I'll . . ." His mouth suddenly clamped shut as a bullet thunked into the ground near his right shoulder.

When the buckboard team jumped into their collars, the wagon lurched forward, dumping Frankie hard onto the seat. Court Nash's bullet went over her head. The lines were wrapped around the brake handle, and were tight enough and pulled hard enough on the snaffle bits in the horses' mouths that they couldn't run. All they could do was jump and snort, first one lunging into its collar, then the other. The wagon was moving in jerks.

Nash fired another shot just as the wagon lurched, and Frankie heard the ugly whine of the lead going past her right ear. Quickly, she thumbed the hammer back on the big pistol in her hands, pointed it in Nash's direction, squeezed her eyes shut, and pulled the trigger.

That shot, right behind the horses, had them wild with fear. They pulled so hard on the bits that a bridle broke. Then they were off. Frankie dropped the gun and unwrapped the lines from the brake handle. She put her feet against the dashboard for leverage, pulled back on the lines, and talked to the horses.

"Who-o-a. Whoa, boys. Who-o-a, now."

The two riders believed there was only one man in the draw, and they split up, one coming from the east and the other from the west. Between them, they'd get him. The rider on the east fired a shot to fetch the sheriff's attention and give the other a chance to get closer. He got the sheriff's attention, but the other rider didn't get any closer. Johnny saw him coming, raised the Dragoon. The rider saw Johnny. Both men believed the first to shoot had the better chance at survival. Both fired hastily. Both missed. Johnny cursed himself for wasting a shot. The horseman bailed off his horse and used the animal as a shield while he tried to get another shot at Johnny.

On the east, the gunman heard the shooting, saw his partner standing and taking aim, and thought the sheriff was being attacked from the west. He spurred his horse right at the draw, firing as he came. His aim from the back of a running horse wasn't good enough. Sheriff Rathke ignored the lead slamming into the ground around him, squinted down the barrel of his sixgun, and squeezed the trigger.

Then there was a saddled horse running free while its rider lay still on the ground.

Seeing his partner shot off his horse, the man on the west holstered his gun, got mounted and rode off at a hard gallop, heading south. That left one gunman. He too saw what happened, got on his horse, and joined the other rider.

The two of them rode through the stolen herd on a gallop and kept going south.

Sheriff Rathke started to say something to Johnny, but Johnny was up and running. He ran toward the barn, almost out of his mind with fear. The women were over there. Court Nash was over there. Court Nash would kill anyone who got in his way. He stopped running when he saw the stampeding team go past the barn with Frankie on the buckboard seat, hauling back on the lines. He could do nothing more than watch as Frankie got the horses slowed to a walk and then to a stop.

Breaking into a run again, Johnny pounded up to the wagon. "I heard shooting," he said, breathless. "What happened?"

Frankie was calm. "One of them shot at us. He shot Mr. Hutchison. I think something broke up there, Johnny."

Sure enough, the snaffle bit was dangling from a broken cheek piece on the off horse. "Hold them," Johnny said. He unhooked the horses from their singletrees, let the end of the wagon tongue drop from a ring on the neck yoke, then led the team away from the wagon. Frankie climbed down and held the horses by the headstalls. Johnny looked over the sideboard at Suzanne.

"Suzie . . . my God, Suzie, are you still alive?"

"Yes," Suzanne said from her cot. "I'm all right." She tried to sit up. "What in the world was going on? Did you get hurt? Is anyone shot?"

"Some men were shot. The sheriff from Cheyenne is here. But we're all right, you, me, and Frankie."

"Thank God." Suzanne fell back on her cot.

"We'll have to fix a headstall, then we'll be on our way. We'll be home soon."

Chapter Twenty-eight

While Frankie stayed with the wagon and Suzanne, Johnny led the team back to the barn. Hutchison had his shirt off, examining his wound. Blood ran down his right arm and dripped off his fingers. Court Nash was sitting on the ground, holding his left leg in both hands, rocking on his rump, groaning in pain.

Ignoring him, Johnny asked Hutchison, "Hurt bad?" The lean, stringy man tried to keep his face straight. "Looks like the ball cut a little piece out of my arm. I reckon I'll live."

Squatting in front of Nash, picking up his gun, Johnny said, "You know me, don't you, Court?"

Grimacing with pain, the short man said, "No. Well, yeah."

"Sure you do. For the past three years I've been looking over my shoulder for you and your killer brother. I won't have to do that anymore."

"I'm hurt, Vorhes. Hurt bad."

"Tough."

"He's the one that shot me," Hutchison said. "But I reckon we'll do what we can for him. Was that a sheriff over there?"

"Yeah, Floyd Rathke, from Cheyenne. He's alive. Here he comes."

Sheriff Rathke walked around a corner of the barn. "Anybody shot over here?"

"Two shot, but alive," Johnny answered. When the lawman came closer, Johnny said, "Tell Bert Goodfellow, when you get back to Cheyenne, that we got the two who shot him. In case you don't know who they are, this one here is Court Nash. The big son-of-a-bitch over there is Powell Nash. They use to be my neighbors."

"No." Rathke was incredulous. "Them?"

"Yup. You just shot hell out of the Nash gang." To Hutchison, Johnny said, "You owe me another bridle."

"Take any of 'em."

He found a bridle in the barn, put it on the off horse's head, rerigged the lines. He started to lead the team back to the buckboard.

"Where you going, Vorhes?"

"Home. I've got a sick woman in the wagon."

"Where's home?"

"East of Rollinsville a ways, on Wild Horse Creek."

"You've got a sick woman, you say?"

"Yep."

"You can go, then. I'll take care of this mess."

Johnny couldn't keep the sarcasm out of his voice. "Thank you kindly for your permission." He started to go on, then stopped and looked back. "Maybe you were right, Sheriff, about the law. I'll give it some thought."

Finally, with the horses hitched to the singletrees again, Johnny climbed to the seat. He looked back at his sister and at Frankie, who was sitting on a satchel next to the cot.

"We have to get her to bed, Johnny, as soon as we can."

"We'll be there before sundown," Johnny said. He clucked to the team, and the buckboard rolled forward.

"Yeah, we're going home now."

Prepare Yourself for

PATRICIA WALLACE

LULLABYE (2917, $3.95/$4.95)
Eight-year-old Bronwyn knew she wasn't like other girls. She didn't have a mother. At least, not a real one. Her mother had been in a coma at the hospital for as long as Bronwyn could remember. She couldn't feel any pain, her father said. But when Bronwyn sat with her mother, she knew her mother was angry—angry at the nurses and doctors, and her own helplessness. Soon, she would show them all the true meaning of suffering . . .

MONDAY'S CHILD (2760, $3.95/$4.95)
Jill Baker was such a pretty little girl, with long, honey-blond hair and haunting gray-green eyes. Just one look at her angelic features could dispel all the nasty rumors that had been spreading around town. There were all those terrible accidents that had begun to plague the community, too. But the fact that each accident occurred after little Jill had been angered had to be coincidence . . .

SEE NO EVIL (2429, $3.95/$4.95)
For young Caryn Dearborn, the cornea operation enabled her to see more than light and shadow for the first time. For Todd Reynolds, it was his chance to run and play like other little boys. For these two children, the sudden death of another child had been the miracle they had been waiting for. But with their eyesight came another kind of vision—of evil, horror, destruction. They could see into other people's minds, their worst fears and deepest terrors. And they could see the gruesome deaths that awaited the unwary . . .

THRILL (3142, $4.50/$5.50)
It was an amusement park like no other in the world. A tri-level marvel of modern technology enhanced by the special effects wizardry of holograms, lasers, and advanced robotics. Nothing could go wrong—until it did. As the crowds swarmed through the gates on Opening Day, they were unprepared for the disaster about to strike. Rich and poor, young and old would be taken for the ride of their lives, trapped in a game of epic proportions where only the winners survived . . .

Available wherever paperbacks are sold, or order direct from the Publisher. Send cover price plus 50¢ per copy for mailing and handling to Zebra Books, Dept. 4095, 475 Park Avenue South, New York, N.Y. 10016. Residents of New York and Tennessee must include sales tax. DO NOT SEND CASH. For a free Zebra/ Pinnacle catalog please write to the above address.